A LAST STAND?

They both turned and looked at Roper. They both knew that if they didn't get him out of there and to a hospital he might die. Dragging him from the Greek Hotel had aggravated his wound, but at least it had stopped bleeding—for now.

"We can't just wait," Clint finally said. "We've got to act."

"Okay," Bat said. "One inside and one outside. Who's going out?"

"Me," Clint said.

Clint peered out his window. The moon was not full, but it was giving off some light. It would not be pitch dark out there, not once his eyes adjusted to having the lamp extinguished inside. When he was able to make out shapes and sizes outside he moved toward the door. With no light inside, he might just be able to open it and slip out without being seen.

"Ready?" he asked Bat.

"I'm ready if you are."

Clint opened the door . . .

THE GUNSMITH

223

BARON OF CRIME

J. R. ROBERTS

JOVE BOOKS, NEW YORK

BARON OF CRIME

A Jove Book / published by arrangement with the author

PRINTING HISTORY
Jove edition / July 2000

The Penguin Putnam Inc. World Wide Web site address is
http://www.penguinputnam.com

ISBN: 0-515-12873-2

A JOVE BOOK®
Jove Books are published by The Berkley Publishing Group,
a division of Penguin Putnam Inc.,
375 Hudson Street, New York, New York 10014.
JOVE and the ''J'' design
are trademarks belonging to Penguin Putnam Inc.

PRINTED IN THE UNITED STATES OF AMERICA

10 9 8 7 6 5 4 3 2 1

PROLOGUE

A Walker Colt was the only gun Fat Gator could find that had a trigger guard that would fit his finger. Any other gun he'd ever had, he'd had to saw off the trigger guard so he could pull the trigger. Once he found the Walker Colt, though, that was the only gun he would use.

Fat Gator was fat. He wasn't just fat, he was incredibly fat. He was so fat that he couldn't travel. He couldn't fit in a stagecoach or board a train without a lot of help. And he hadn't been able to ride a horse since he was twelve years old. His parents starting calling him Gator right from the day he was born, and from the time he was ten he was Fat Gator. They both said he looked like a Gator from right out of the Bayou, and his siblings took up the chant when they got old enough. He was Fat Gator to his brother, sisters, and his parents, right up until the day, at fifteen, he had killed them all, torched the family home, and took off on his own, leaving Louisiana behind him forever.

He spent the next twenty years educating himself and get fatter at the same time. By the time he had become too fat to travel he had a ranch outside of El Paso, Texas, where he raised horses—or, rather, his foreman and his

1

men raised horses. He spent most of his time planning robberies and sending "the twins" out to pull them off.

He had an elaborate network which he used to collect information from all around the country. He knew when a big payroll was being transported and how or when a bank had a huge deposit in its safe, and he managed to get maps and diagrams delivered to him so he could make his plans.

It had taken him years to get himself set up this way. All he had been lacking for a long time was personnel he could trust to go out and put his plans into effect properly. He found them when he found the twins.

Of course, they weren't twins, really. They weren't related and looked nothing alike. What they had in common, though, was a background of hard times and a thirst for better ones. Once he found them, spoke to them, educated them, and put them together, he had the last piece of his puzzle. He surrounded them with people who were good at doing what they were told, and then launched his career in crime. Fat Gator and the twins had been successful at it for three years, now.

He was a rich man and didn't need the money he made from the robberies. That is, he didn't need it to live, but he did need it to feed his ego and to pay the twins, so he kept it in a safe place on his ranch and did not mix it with the money in the bank, which he had "earned" legitimately.

As for the name Fat Gator, that now existed only in his head. Nobody called him that anymore, because nobody knew about it. He kept it in his head just to remind himself of where he had come from—a place where his parents told him he'd never amount to anything and would always just be Fat Gator—a nobody, a nothing, a laughingstock, a joke.

Too bad they were dead and couldn't see just how wrong they had been.

ONE

Clint looked across the table at his friend, Talbot Roper. They were in one of Roper's favorite Denver restaurants, Madonna's Steakhouse. Clint looked around a bit. There were no Madonna statues and, in fact, no religious icons to be seen anywhere, which he mentioned.

"And there won't be," Roper said. "The place is owned by a man named Mike Madonna."

"A friend?"

"Hardly," Roper said.

"Then why do you eat here?"

"The food is excellent."

"Well," Clint said, "I can't argue with you there."

"So, do you want to hear my theory or not?"

"How long have you been working on it?"

"Years."

"How many years?"

"Maybe two," Roper said, "but I think the crimes go back a year before that."

"All right," Clint said, "entertain me."

"Three years of major robberies," Roper said. "Banks, stagecoaches, trains, payrolls, every kind you could imag-

3

ine. All meticulously planned and carried out."

"By the same people?"

"That's my theory."

"Who?"

"That I don't know."

"Why?"

"Well, the obvious answer would be for the money."

Clint sipped his wine and put his glass down. "But you've never been one to accept the obvious answer, have you, Tal?"

"You know me well."

"So then, why?"

"I think," Roper said, "because he can."

"One man?" Clint asked. "You think these jobs have been pulled by just one man?"

"No," Roper said, "I think they've been planned by just one man. Pulled off by a gang, but planned by one man."

"Why do you think that?"

"Because they're all so brilliantly planned," Roper said, "and I'd hate to think there's more than one crook out there who's that smart."

"So what's your best guess?" Clint asked. "Who is it?"

Roper shrugged. "I don't have a guess. I'm still looking. But I do know one thing."

"What's that?"

"He's put a crack crew together to pull these jobs off," Roper said.

"You've got something up your sleeve, Tal," Clint said. "Why else would you send for me?"

"To buy you dinner?"

"The food was good," Clint said, looking at the remnants of their meal in front of them on the table, "but not that good. I didn't come here from Labyrinth, Texas, for this."

"No," Roper said, "you didn't." He leaned forward. "I want to set a trap."

"What kind of trap?"

"The kind these people won't be able to resist."

"You're talking about big money."

"That's right."

"How big?"

"Half a million, maybe," Roper said. "How could they resist that?"

"Half a million," Clint said, thoughtfully. "That'd have to be a government payroll, or at least a government project. You think they'd bother with something like that, that was bound to be protected by the army?"

Roper scratched his jaw.

"Maybe you're right," Roper said. "Maybe that's too big. You see why I need you?"

"You're going to need a lot of cooperation to pull this off, Tal," Clint said. "If these people research their jobs before they pull them, you're going to have to convince them it's real. You can't just plant a story in a newspaper."

"I know that," Roper said. "We'll just have to come up with some kind of a plan."

"We?"

"I need your help, Clint," Roper said. "I can't do this without you."

"Let me ask you something."

"What?"

"Why do you want to do it at all?" Clint asked. "You're a private detective. Catching these people, that's something for the law to do—or do you have a client?"

Roper didn't answer.

"You do," Clint said, after a moment. "You have a client, and it's somebody with big money."

"Want some coffee?" Roper asked.

"Do we still have some things to talk about?"

"Yes."

"Then I want coffee."

Roper raised his hand and called the waiter over, ordered coffee. Before they could resume their conversation, however, a man came walking over to their table. He was well dressed in a black suit and tie, a white shirt, and—Clint could see by the bulge under his jacket—was wearing a gun in a shoulder rig.

"And who's this?" Clint asked, as the man came closer.

"Nobody," Roper said, but he continued to stare at the man until he actually reached their table.

TWO

"Good evening, Roper," the man said.

"What do you want, Madonna?"

"Well," Madonna said, spreading his hands, "Denver's most respected detective is eating in my restaurant, I just thought I'd come over and say hello."

"There's no need for that," Roper said. "I come here for the food, Madonna, not the company."

Madonna ignored Roper after that and turned his attention to Clint.

"I'm sorry, but Talbot is obviously not going to introduce us," the man said. "I am Michael Madonna, and this is my restaurant."

"Clint Adams," Clint said. He was not exactly sure how he was supposed to be reacting, and Roper was giving him no clues.

"Ah, the famous Gunsmith," Madonna said. "I had heard that you and Talbot Roper were friends. What a legendary pair."

"What do you want, Madonna?" Roper demanded again.

"I told you, Talbot," Madonna said, "I just came over to say hello."

7

"Well, you've said it," Roper said, "and I'll thank you not to call me by my first name. That's a right that is reserved for my friends."

Now Madonna looked at Roper again.

"Well, excuse me, Mr. Roper," Madonna said. "In the future I'll remember that. You, uh, will be dining here in the future?"

"Unfortunately," Roper said, "you have one of the three best kitchens in Denver, so the answer is yes."

"One of the three best?" Madonna said, with interest. "I thought I had the best. What are the other two establishments?"

"I don't think I'll say."

"Why not?"

"They might find themselves on the wrong end of a fire bomb," Roper said, looking directly into Madonna's eyes.

Madonna held Talbot's stare for a few moments, then looked at Clint Adams, amusement on his face.

"Your friend," he said to Clint, "is such a kidder sometimes. I hope you enjoyed your dinner?"

"It was excellent."

"I'll send over some dessert, gentlemen," Madonna said. "Enjoy it."

With that Michael Madonna turned and walked away, began glad-handing patrons at other tables.

"Well," Roper said, "that was awkward."

"If you don't like the man," Clint said, "why do you eat here?"

"Like I said," Roper replied, "he has one of the three best kitchens in this city."

"What *are* the other two?" Clint asked.

"I'll tell you after we leave here."

"That stuff about fire bombs—"

"Rumors," Talbot said, "innuendo . . . nothing was ever proven."

"But you think—"

"I think I don't want to talk about Mike Madonna right now," Talbot said. "Can we get back on the subject?"

"You had the floor," Clint said. "I was just waiting."

"It's not going to be so easy to plant something," Roper said, about twenty minutes later. "There's not a general area of operation for this gang, except that they stay west of the Mississippi. They've pulled jobs in New Mexico, Missouri, Minnesota, all over."

"Maybe," Clint said, "you should look for someplace they haven't pulled a job, yet."

"See?" Roper said, smiling. "See why I want your help? I'll go back into my files and take a look. Okay, we'll plant a story about a huge payroll and use a state they haven't hit, yet."

"We?"

"Come on, Clint," Roper said, "don't keep me in suspense. Are you going to help me or not?"

"Of course I'm going to help you, Tal," Clint said. "I wouldn't have come if I wasn't, would I?"

THREE

Clint and Talbot Roper agreed to meet in the lobby of Clint's hotel, the Denver House, the next morning to have breakfast and further discuss their temporary partnership. Roper walked Clint to the hotel, but did not go in.

"I'm going home to turn in," Roper said. "I want to get an early start tomorrow morning."

"There's one thing I didn't ask you, Tal."

"I know," Roper said. "Who my client is."

"Right."

"Let's leave that for tomorrow, all right?"

"Fine."

Clint knew that Roper needed some time to consider the question, and whether or not he could answer it without compromising his ethics. He was willing to give his friend that time.

"Heading for the hotel bar?" Roper asked Clint.

"No," Clint said, "I'm making it an early night, too." He had just gotten off the train that afternoon and had barely had time to catch his breath.

"Good," Roper said, "then let's make it nine A.M. in the lobby."

"Nine A.M. it is."

The two men shook hands warmly, friends for a long time, partners every so often, and now again.

"Thanks for coming, Clint."

"You knew I would," Clint said. "That's why you asked."

Roper smiled, then walked away, shaking his head. Clint waited until his friend was out of sight, then turned and went into the hotel.

He stayed at the Denver House whenever he was in Denver, and they always had one of the best rooms for him. It was a two-room suite, with indoor facilities. Once in the room he wouldn't have to leave again for any reason, if he didn't want to.

He removed the Colt New Line from his belt and set it down on the end table near the bed. His gun belt was also hanging on the bedpost, where he could get at it quickly. A man in his position could never have too many guns close at hand.

He removed his boots, socks, and shirt and was considering whether or not he wanted a bath when there was a knock at the door. He wondered if Talbot Roper had forgotten to cover something with him. Just in case, though, he took the New Line with him to the door.

Whoever was at the door began to knock again just as he opened it. The woman in the hall gasped and took a step back.

"Y-you startled me," she said, accusingly.

"I'm sorry," Clint said. "I didn't know—I didn't mean to. Who are you?"

She put her hand to her chest and said, "Please, give me a chance to get my breath back."

She was wearing a gown with a shawl over her shoulders. However, when she took a deep breath it swelled her breasts so that they threatened to spill from the low-cut neckline of her dress. She was tall, dark-haired, pale of skin, and very well endowed, and Clint found watching her attempts to regain her breath to be a great pleasure.

"You're staring," she said, then.

"I know," he said, "and so are you. How do you feel?"

"Better."

"Then maybe you can tell me who you are?"

"A friend," she said.

"Of whose?"

"Well," she said, "for tonight, of yours."

"Did the hotel—"

"No," she said, "I was sent up to keep you company by a mutual friend."

"Who?"

"He said to tell you that no matter what," she said, "he still expects you to meet him in the lobby at nine A.M."

Roper.

She looked him up and down and said, "I'd say your chances of that would be about fifty-fifty."

He smiled at her and said, "I'll take those odds."

"May I come in?'

He stepped back and said, "By all means."

FOUR

Clint didn't make it to the lobby until nine forty-five.

The girl's name was Ginger. She was in her late twenties and her body, though full, was firm with no sag anywhere that he could see—and he saw everywhere.

When she came in she simply smiled at him and dropped the shawl and dress to the floor.

"Consider me a present," she'd said, spreading her arms wide. This was a girl who liked the way she looked. Spreading her arms like that lifted her full breasts, the nipples of which were already distended. He also liked that she made no effort to suck in her belly, which was not flat, but who cared. He never liked a flat belly on a woman, he'd always preferred a woman with some meat and some weight on her.

Ginger had both, and she was tall enough to carry them well.

"Well," Clint said, "I was never one to look a gift horse in the mouth, but I usually like to unwrap my own presents."

"Too late," she said, and leaped toward him so he had to catch her. They fell onto the bed that way, with her on

15

top of him, and he enjoyed the feel of all that hot, naked flesh lying on him. She kissed him, her tongue just flicking in and out of his mouth, fluttering like the wings of a bird rather than darting straight into his mouth like a snake.

He kissed her back, slid his hands down until he was cupping the cheeks of her ample backside. She moaned into his mouth as he slid one finger along the crease between her cheeks. Abruptly, he turned her over so that she was on the bottom and began to roam about her body with his mouth. Somewhere along the way he managed to shuck his clothes and then he was on top of her and inside of her where it was hot and steamy and slick and then she was groaning and crying out, wrapping her powerful legs around him and raking his back with her nails . . .

"Wow," she said, the next morning. They had gone at each other three more times during the night, like two starving people. "I feel like I got the present."

"No" he said, "believe me, it was me who got the gift— and what a gift it was."

He stroked her right thigh with his hand and she shivered.

"I swear," she said, "wherever you touch me it feels like . . . well, like it never felt before."

He moved his hand from her thigh, over her belly, and then down between her legs, where she was still wet and waiting.

That's why he was late . . .

"How did you like your present?" Roper asked when he finally appeared in the hotel lobby.

"She was great," Clint said. "Is she a pro?"

"A friend," Roper said. "I know how you feel about pros."

"I love them," Clint said, "I just don't want to pay them."

"Did you leave her in your room?"

"Yes," Clint said. "Asleep."

"Well," Roper said, "as long as you don't have anything of real value in there."

Clint glanced at him sharply, then realized his friend was kidding.

"Come on," Roper said, "I've got a good place to take you for breakfast."

"Is it owned by Mike Madonna?"

"No."

"Or somebody else you don't like?"

"Don't worry," Roper said. "This is one of my favorite places, owned by one of my favorite people."

"Okay, fine," Clint said. "Lead the way."

"Sure you got your legs under you?"

Clint's legs did feel a bit weak from all the activity with Ginger, but he said, "You lead the way and I'll follow, don't worry."

They left the hotel and started walking west. They went five or six blocks and then Roper took him into a small café. Inside was dark, with drawn curtains and dark furnishings.

"What's that I smell?" Clint asked.

"Whatever you want it to be," Roper said. "They cook anything for you, here."

"For me or for you?"

Roper smiled.

"You're with me, so it's the same thing."

"This place must be owned by a woman."

Roper clapped his friend on the shoulder and said, "You should be a detective."

A waiter came over, greeted Roper by name, and showed them to a table in the back of the place. Clint counted about twenty tables, half of which were taken.

"It's a popular place for breakfast," Roper said, as they sat, "but it's still a little early."

"What can I get for you and our friend, Mr. Roper?"

"Coffee, right?" Roper said to Clint.

"Right."

"Coffee to start, Alfred."

"Yes, sir."

"Is Mrs. Foster here yet, Alfred?"

"Yes, sir," Alfred said. "She's in her office. I'll tell her you're here, I'm sure she'll want to come out and say hello."

"Very good."

"*Mrs.* Foster?" Clint asked.

"A widow, the poor woman. Her husband died two years ago and left her this place."

"Were you and her husband friends?"

"I never met the man."

"How did you and Mrs. Foster meet?"

"She hired me last year to clear up some business for her."

"What kind of business?"

Roper made a face and said, "Nasty business."

"Ah," Clint said, "blackmail," but Roper wouldn't bite.

"You're a steak and eggs man, if I remember correctly," he said, instead. "Great steak and eggs here."

"I'll take your word for it, then," Clint said. "That's what I'll order."

Alfred returned with a coffeepot and two cups. He set the cups down, filled them, and then set the pot down.

"And for breakfast?" he asked.

Roper signaled for Clint to go first, so he said, "Steak and eggs."

"And with that, sir?"

"Whatever trappings you see fit to add to it will be fine," Clint said.

"Very well, sir. And you, Mr. Roper?"

"The same, Alfred, but make sure we get a nice big basket of hot biscuits, all right?"

"Of course, sir."

"Alfred?"

"Yes, sir?"

"Did you tell Mrs. Foster we were here?"

"Yes, sir. She'll be out momentarily."

The waiter walked away and Clint asked, "Why do I get the feeling he doesn't like you?"

"Too polite, right?"

"Way too polite."

"I think he's in love with Virginia."

"And Virginia would be Mrs. Foster?"

"That's right."

"Well . . . he's sixty if he's a day," Clint said. "How old is this merry widow of yours?"

"You know what?" Roper said. "I've always been too much of a gentleman to ask."

Clint had to admit that as well as his friend did with the women, he usually did it while being a gentleman.

"Well," he said, "maybe when she appears I'll be able to hazard a guess or two about her age."

"Do me a favor, then," Roper said.

"What?"

"Don't do it out loud."

FIVE

Over breakfast Roper outlined his idea for their plan, but before Clint could contribute Roper saw a woman walking across the floor toward them.

"Here she comes," he said.

"Who?" Clint asked.

"Virginia Foster."

Clint turned his head to look. An elegant-looking woman in her forties was walking toward them with a smile on her face and—he could see as she came closer—a gleam in her eyes.

"Talbot," she said, "how nice of you to come visit. You haven't been here in so long."

Roper stood. The woman gave him her cheek and he kissed it. Up close she was a handsome forty-five or so. An attractive woman with manners, breeding, and looks.

And a widow.

Clint wondered if his friend was suddenly contemplating marriage.

"Virginia," Roper said, "I'd like you to meet my friend, Clint Adams."

Clint stood and took the proffered hand. Virginia Foster

was wearing a dress that covered her from head to toe, leaving nothing bare but her hands. The top of it went all the way up her neck, as if she was trying to hide something—and maybe she was. When Clint took her hand he saw—and felt—that it was not quite as well preserved as the rest of her. He added five or six years to his previous estimation of her age.

"Mr. Adams," she said. "I see you've chosen to dine on our house specialty."

"It's excellent," Clint said.

"The steak is cooked to your satisfaction?"

"Exactly."

"Good," she said. "Well sit down, gentlemen, don't let your breakfast go cold on account of me."

"Would you join us for coffee?" Roper asked.

"Of course."

She sat down and Alfred appeared immediately with a cup and poured for her. While he was there he also filled Clint and Roper's cups, then left.

"What brings you to Denver, Mr. Adams?" she asked.

"Just stopping in to see my old friend," Clint said, indicating Talbot.

She looked at both men in turn and then laughed.

"So you two are doing business together."

"What makes you say that?" Roper asked.

"I don't doubt that you are friends," she said, "but I can't see either one of you taking time out to simply visit one another. You see, Mr. Adams, I am aware of your reputation and, of course, I know how busy Talbot keeps."

Neither man responded.

"All right," she said, "keep your business to yourselves, then. How long will you be in Denver, Mr. Adams?"

"That's not something I'm real sure about, ma'am," Clint said.

"Oh God, please don't call me 'ma'am,' " she said.

"My name is Virginia. Any friend of Talbot's may call me Virginia."

"Thank you, Virginia."

"You shall have to come back to sample some of my chef's dinners," she said, putting her hand on Clint's arm.

"I'll make a point of it."

"And bring your friend," she said, giving Roper a pointed look. "Will I see you later?"

"I'll stop by," Roper said.

She smiled and stood up. She had never touched her coffee.

"It was a pleasure to meet you, Mr. Adams," she said. "Please don't get up. It's not necessary."

"I hope to see you again, ma—Virginia."

"I believe we can probably count on that, Clint," she said. "Good day, gentlemen. Go on back to your business. The lady is leaving."

They watched as she walked back across the room, almost gliding as she did so. She did not stop to speak to any of the other customers.

"What's all that about?" Clint asked.

"All what?"

" 'Will I see you later?' " Clint repeated. "Are you and the lady . . . an item, Mr. Roper?"

"Would it surprise you if we were?"

"Frankly, yes."

"Why? Because of her age?"

"That's one thing," Clint said. "You have to admit, you usually lean toward younger women."

"Well, younger women don't have her class."

"Or her standing in the community."

"What if I was thinking about settling down?" Roper asked. "It wouldn't hurt to have a little standing, would it?"

"I didn't think that was something you worried about,"

Clint said. "Besides, you do have some standing in the community."

"Not in certain circles."

"Again," Clint said, "I didn't think those were circles you cared to travel in socially."

"This isn't getting us anywhere," Roper said. "I just thought you'd be interested to meet her."

"I was," Clint said. "In fact, I found meeting her very interesting."

"Then can we move on to other business?"

"Definitely," Clint said. "I'm all for moving on to other business."

SIX

"Where?"

"Minnesota."

"I vote no."

"Why?" Roper asked.

"Too cold."

"Is that the only reason?"

"The James Boys didn't fare too well there," Clint reminded him. "Might keep another gang from wanting to try it."

"All right, then," Roper said, "on to my second choice."

"Which is?"

"Idaho."

"Idaho? Who goes to Idaho?"

"Exactly."

"Have you ever been to Idaho?" Clint asked.

"Actually," Roper said, "once."

"I've never been there."

"It's not a bad place."

"Is it warmer than Minnesota?"

"Yes."

"Okay," Clint said, "then I have no quarrel with Idaho."

"Good," Roper said, "that's settled. Now we just need to get some cooperation from the powers that be in Idaho."

"Well," Clint said, "that'll be your job."

"We'll both have to go to Idaho, though."

"Why don't you go to Idaho and set it up?" Clint asked. "I'll stay here and hold down the fort."

"There's no fort to hold down, Clint."

"Well, your office—"

"When I leave town I close my office."

"What about your secretary—"

"I give her a vacation."

"Okay, fine, then," Clint said. "We'll both go to Idaho."

"Good," Roper said. "That's settled, too."

"And what about your client?"

"What about him?"

"Whoever he is," Clint asked, "will he be any help to us in getting some cooperation in Idaho?"

"I don't know," Roper said, "I'll have to ask him."

"Why don't we ask him?" Clint asked. "After all, since I'm going to be working with you I'm sure you'll want me to know who our client is."

Roper squirmed uncomfortably.

"He doesn't want you to tell me."

"He doesn't even want me to bring you into this," Roper said.

"But you won that battle, apparently."

"Yes. I can even pay you."

"Oh, well, that'll be nice," Clint said. "It's always nice to get paid when you're doing someone a favor—especially a friend."

"Clint look—"

"I don't remember asking to be paid, Tal."

Roper realized he had made his friend testy.

"I didn't mean it as an insult," Roper said. "I just mean

the client is wealthy, why not make him pay both of us?"

"So he'll pay me, but I can't know who he is."

"No," Roper said, and then, "not yet, anyway."

"When, then?"

"I don't know."

Clint stared across the table at his friend.

"You know, Tal," he said, "if it was anyone else I'd tell them to go fuck themselves."

"I realize that, Clint," Roper said, "and I'm sorry, but I gave my word—I mean, I could tell you anyway, but—"

Clint held up his hands and said, "No, no, no, I'm not going to be the one who makes you break your word."

"Then you'll still help me?"

"Yes," Clint said, "I'll still help."

"Good," Roper said, with relief. "Believe me, it was never my intention to insult you. I mean, if it was just up to me I'd tell you—"

"Tal," Clint said. "Just drop it, okay? It's okay . . . for now."

"Okay, good," Roper said, "fine, it's . . . okay." Clearly, he was still uncomfortable, so Clint took a little solace from that."

They finished their breakfast and paid the waiter, who accepted the money without a word.

Outside on the street Clint said, "I kind of thought breakfast would be on the lady."

"Oh no," Roper said, "she and I may be . . . friends . . . but she's still a businesswoman."

"That's . . . an odd relationship to have."

Roper didn't comment.

"I'll need the rest of the day to send some telegrams and try to make some arrangements," Roper said. "Maybe even tomorrow, but I don't see any reason why we can't leave the day after."

"Fine."

"I'll arrange for train tickets," Roper said, "and horses when we get to the other end of the line—unless, of course, you plan to bring Duke—"

"No Duke," Clint said.

"Why not?"

"The big black has been put out to pasture."

Roper stared at Clint in disbelief.

"It's true."

"I thought that big gelding would go on forever," Roper said.

"So did I."

"So what are you doing for a horse these days?"

"Looking.'

"So then it's okay if I make the arrangements?"

"Go ahead," Clint said. "It's been months and I haven't had any luck in finding a permanent replacement."

"I'm not surprised," Roper said. "What kind of a horse could replace Duke?"

"No kind, up to now," Clint said. "All right, so I'll amuse myself while you send telegrams and make arrangements."

"Let's meet tonight for dinner," Roper said.

"Where?"

"Your hotel, again."

"All right."

"I should know more, then."

"I'll look forward to it," Clint said.

Roper stared at Clint a moment longer, then shook his head and said, "Duke put out to pasture. It shakes your faith."

"Don't rub it in," Clint said.

SEVEN

Clint decided to hit the nearest telegraph office and send a telegram to his friend Rick Hartman, in Labyrinth, Texas. Hartman rarely left Texas anymore, but had a grapevine across the entire United States. He was able to find out almost anything just by the use of the telegraph. If anyone would have information on a gang pulling robberies west of the Mississippi, it would be him.

Roper had not yet told Clint exactly what jobs he was attributing to this gang, so Clint could not be very specific with Hartman. However, he could alert his friend that such information would be forthcoming. Meanwhile, maybe one of Hartman's contacts had made the same discovery that Talbot Roper had made—although, when he thought about it, Clint doubted it. After all, Roper was—to his mind—the best detective in the business. Better than Allan Pinkerton or any of his family or operatives, and better, even, than Clint's other friend, Heck Thomas. For someone else to have made the same discovery, they would have to be as smart as Roper. Clint didn't think there was anyone out there who fit that bill.

He sent the telegram, anyway.

• • •

Also sending a telegram was a man by the name of William Halliday. His telegram was going to El Paso, Texas. Upon its arrival it would be delivered to the ranch owned by Henry Miller. Miller, in his younger years, had been christened "Fat Gator," by his family, but of course, Bill Halliday knew nothing of this.

Halliday was a detective who had been hired by Henry Miller to gather certain information. He had strict instructions not to act on the information, but to simply pass it along and await instructions. Therefore, Halliday's telegram was very short and to the point. It said: YOUR FEARS ARE FOUNDED. AWAITING INSTRUCTIONS.

Halliday sent the telegram and returned to his office, where he would wait all day, if necessary, for the reply to be delivered.

Clint hadn't been in Denver in a while so after sending the telegram he walked and rode around the city, reacquainting himself with some of the sights. He ended up back at his hotel early in the evening. He decided to have dinner there, as he and Roper had agreed that they would meet late and would each have dinner on their own.

He went to his room first, however, to freshen up. When he opened it the first thing he noticed was the scent in the air. It was the scent left behind by Ginger. He knew it was just the remnants of her visit because it was not fresh or strong enough for her to still be there—not that he would have minded.

He went into the bedroom and found that the maid had made the bed and changed the sheets. Ginger's scent was in the air, but it would no longer be in the bed. Clint doubted that she'd be back. He didn't think Roper would arrange for another night. He was sorry he hadn't asked the girl where she lived, or how to get in touch with her, but then what for? If things went as planned, he and Roper would be leaving Denver day after tomorrow and heading for Idaho.

Idaho.

He'd never had any reason to go there and, frankly, never thought he would. But then again, at least it wasn't Minnesota.

He decided to take a bath, since he had all the makings of a nice hot one right in his room. After a good soak his appetite would be piqued and he'd be ready for a nice big dinner.

Bill Halliday answered the knock on his door. It was a runner from the telegraph office with his reply. It was about time. His stomach was growling furiously.

The reply read: ACT WITHIN 24 HOURS. WILL AWAIT THE OUTCOME.

He folded the telegram. He knew exactly what it meant. Had he been a reputable private detective he wouldn't have known, but he had not been that for a very long time, now.

First, though, he was going to eat.

Henry Miller sat back in his custom-made chair. He had the chair made in St. Louis and transported to El Paso. It was the only chair he knew he could sit in comfortably, and it would bear his weight. He decided to keep the chair behind his desk, because he spent most of the time in the room he used as an office.

At the moment he was sitting back in the chair, staring at the man standing across from him. The man's name was Joe Pittman, and he was one of the twins.

"Did you send the reply?" he asked.

"I did."

"Good."

"Are you sure you don't want us to go to Denver and handle it ourselves?" Pittman asked.

"No," Miller said. "Of all the things you are, you are not professional killers. It will be handled by professionals."

"Can you tell me again why you think this detective, Talbot Roper, is a danger to us?"

"Because," Miller said, folding his hands across the corpulent stomach, "he is, quite simply, the best detective in the country, and I heard that he's been asking questions."

"About us?" Pittman asked. "How could he know?"

"He doesn't know," Miler said. "He doesn't know a damned thing, for sure, that's why he's been asking questions."

"About us?"

"About some of the jobs we've successfully pulled off."

"But we've successfully pulled off every job you've planned."

"I realize that," the former "Fat Gator" replied, "but as of now he's only asked about some of them. I want him dealt with before he asks about more of them."

"I see."

"I know you do," Miller said. "You're very smart, Joseph. The man is a danger to us. We'll have to temporarily suspend our operations if he's not dealt with soon."

"Suspend?" Pittman asked. "What about the Sacramento job?"

"We can wait a few days," Miller said, "or even weeks, if we have to. The both of you could probably use a vacation."

"We don't want a vacation," Pittman said. "We want to work."

"Do you speak for both of you?"

"I do."

"All right, then," Miller said. "We'll see."

"That's it?"

Miller smiled and said, "Don't be impatient—don't either of you get impatient. Continue to do as I say and everything will be fine. All right?"

"Yes," Pittman said, "all right."

"Because I always make it fine, don't I?"

"Yes, you do."

"Yes," Henry "Fat Gator" Miller said, sitting back in his chair, "I do."

EIGHT

After his bath Clint put on some fresh clothes and went down to the hotel dining room for dinner. As he reached the lobby he saw Ginger entering through the front door and walking toward him. He stopped and smiled, and she smiled back.

"Don't get the wrong idea," she said, right away.

"What idea would that be?" he asked.

"That Roper sent me again, tonight."

"He didn't?"

"No, I'm here on my own."

"And why is that?"

"Because I knew you'd like to buy me dinner."

"Oh, you knew that, huh?"

"Yes," Ginger said. "Do you know what else I know?"

"No, what?"

"That we'd both like to find out some more about each other," she said. "I mean, relate to each other out of bed as well as in . . . or am I wrong?"

"No, you're not wrong," Clint said. "I'd be very interested in learning more about you, but—"

"But you don't want me to get the wrong idea?"

35

"Exactly."

"Well, don't worry," Ginger said. "I don't expect forever and a picket fence from a man just because he asks me something about myself."

"Well, all right then," Clint said, extending his arm. "Would you like to join me for dinner, Miss—"

"Tompkins," she said. "My full name is Ginger Tompkins, and I would love to join you for dinner, Mr. Adams."

She took his arm and they went into the dining room together.

Talbot Roper had lived as long as he had by paying attention to his instincts. As he came out of his office late that afternoon, locking it behind him, his instincts told him to look behind him. As he did he saw the sun reflecting off a shiny surface, and he threw himself down on the ground just as a bullet whizzed over his head and imbedded itself in the wooden door. Actually, if he hadn't dropped to the ground the bullet would not have gone over his head, it would have struck him *in* the head.

Even as he hit the ground Roper was hoping that the shooter was working alone. If there were two shooters, both professionals, then the second one was drawing a bead on him even now, and . . . he was too late. The second shot came and the bullet struck him high up on the left shoulder, hitting him in the back. Two pros, and he was in serious trouble if he didn't get off the street.

He got to his feet and launched himself at his office door, striking it with the uninjured shoulder. It was a sturdy door, built and installed to withstand forced entry, but his desperation gave him strength and the door gave on the first try and flew open. He fell inside, stayed on the floor, drawing his gun.

This was better. His shoulder was numb, and he didn't

know how badly he was hit, but it was better to be inside than out on the street. Now they would have to decide whether to come and get him, or to be satisfied with the one good shot. For all they knew, the one wound would finish him off.

For that matter, it might, for all *he* knew, as well.

Clint and Ginger talked over dinner, exchanging stories. She had been living in Denver for only a couple of years, having come there from back East. She didn't say exactly where in the east she was from, and he didn't ask. It seemed the kind of thing she might have left out on purpose.

When it came to talking about what she did for a living she said, "I'm trying to earn enough money to open my own shop."

"What kind of shop?"

"A millinery shop."

"Ah."

There was an awkward moment between them and then she said, "You're wondering what I'm doing to earn it, aren't you? Wondering if I do what we did last night?"

"Well—"

"Talbot asked me to come and see you," she said, "meet you, take a look at you, whatever. But what happened after that was entirely up to me. If I didn't like you, I was free to turn around a leave."

"I see."

"But I didn't leave," she said, "because I liked you."

"And I appreciate the fact that you didn't leave."

She seemed to be making excuses for herself for having taken money to sleep with him. She needn't have bothered, but he didn't tell her that. If she wanted to explain it away, let her. That was her business.

Or it wasn't. Whatever it was, it was her own affair.

After that they talked a bit about his reputation.

"What do you know about it?" he asked.

"Well, Talbot told me," she said, "but then I went and did some research on my own."

"What kind of research?"

"Old newspaper."

"You can't believe what people put in newspapers."

"I know that," she said. "I figured it was all about half true, if that."

"And how did you intend to find out?"

"From you."

"And you'll believe what I tell you about my, uh, reputation?"

She put her elbows on the table, her chin in her hands and said, "Every word."

Roper started awake, realizing that he had either fallen asleep or passed out. Either way he might never have awakened if the two shooters had come across the street to check on him. They could have walked right in on him and shot him dead while he lay on the floor, unconscious.

He felt warm, and the shoulder hurt like hell, now. Apparently, though, the shooters had decided not to beard him in his own den, so to speak. He had to be sure, though, that they weren't still out there, waiting.

There had been two shots. Perhaps not enough of them for someone to have sent for the police. After all, his office had been in this neighborhood for a while, and he had been shot at before.

He got to his knees and crawled to the doorway, gun in hand. The door was open, but it was still securely fastened to the doorjamb by its hinges. That was good, at least he would not have to replace the door, hinges, and lock, just the lock.

He peered outside, checking the buildings across the

street. He believed the shots had come from one of the rooftops. He stared at them for a few moments, and detected no movement. He thought they were gone, but of course, he wouldn't know for sure until he tried to step outside. However, before he could try he passed out again.

NINE

It was getting late, and Clint was getting worried. It wasn't like Talbot Roper to miss an appointment.

"Are you sure he said tonight?" Ginger asked.

"I'm positive."

They were sitting in the lobby, waiting for Roper. Ginger wanted to say hi, but then said she would go up to Clint's room to wait for him—if that was all right with him. He said it definitely was.

"Something's wrong," Clint said. "There's been trouble."

"Maybe you're jumping to conclusions."

"Maybe not," Clint said, as he saw the uniformed police officer enter the lobby of the hotel.

Ginger went to Clint's room while he went with the policeman to a nearby hospital. He found Roper being treated for a gunshot wound to the shoulder. He'd been shot from behind.

"Sonofabitch," Clint said.

Roper, lying on his stomach while a doctor treated the wound, said, "It looks worse than it is."

"Like hell it does," the doctor said. "This is a bad wound, Roper."

Roper looked up at the police officer and said, "Thanks for bringing him, Danny boy."

"No problem, Mr. Roper," the officer said. "You can count on me." He was young, in his twenties, and obviously impressed with Roper.

"Have you reported this?" Clint asked, as the policeman left.

"Yeah, there was a detective here."

"Where did this happen?"

"Outside my office," Roper said. "I was just locking up."

"How many?"

"Two shooters," Roper said, "and they were professional, Clint. I sensed something was wrong and went down. The first shot missed me but the second didn't. They were ready for me."

"No follow up?"

"I got off the street and back into my office," Roper said. "I guess they didn't want to come in after me."

"If their aim was to incapacitate you," the doctor said, "there was no reason for them to stay around. They succeeded."

"Just patch me up, Doc," Roper said, "and bandage me nice and tight."

"You don't think you're leaving this hospital today, do you?" the doctor asked.

"What do you think?'

"Over my dead body," the doctor said. "I've spent a lot of time patching you up, Roper, and I'll be damned if I'll let you go out and ruin my work. You're staying here overnight."

"Like hell—"

"Don't worry, Doc," Clint said, cutting his friend off. "He's staying."

"You think?" Roper asked.

"I know," Clint said, "or I'm on the next train out of here."

Roper craned his neck to look at Clint.

"You're serious."

"Dead serious."

Roper blew some air out his mouth, making a disgusted sound.

"Get me a bed, Doc," he said, "but only for the night."

"After that you'll have to stay home awhile," the doctor added.

"We'll see about that," Roper replied.

"I'm going to wait outside until he finishes patching you up and gives you a room," Clint said, "and then we'll talk some more."

"Fine," Roper said. "We can figure out a way to get me out of here—oh, wait, you went and joined the enemy."

"Just shut up and let the man work," Clint said.

"Thank you," the doctor said.

"You're welcome."

"Can you two make friends later, please?" Roper asked.

"I'll wait outside, Tal," Clint said, and went out into the hall.

There was no way Talbot Roper was going to be able to go to Idaho day after tomorrow, Clint knew. That meant that he had to come up with an alternate plan. One that would work and would keep Roper from trying to get on a train. By the time the doctor came out to say he was finished, he thought he had one.

"They'll be taking him to a room, now," the doctor said to Clint. "If you're his friend you'll find a way to im-

mobilize him for a week or so—and not let him go back
to work for at least three weeks."

"I'll try, Doc. How's he doing?"

"The wound actually could have been worse," the man
said. "But it still did a lot of damage. He's got a lot of
healing to do, plus right now he's got a fever."

"Can I talk to him?"

"Let them take him up and get him comfortable," the
doctor said, "and then he's all yours—but not for long.
He needs his rest."

"Yes, sir," Clint said. "Whatever you say."

"I just wish your friend had the same attitude."

TEN

When Clint entered Roper's room he saw his friend lying on his stomach in bed. It looked like a very uncomfortable position.

Roper's head was turned toward the door so he saw Clint as soon as he entered.

"This is your fault," Roper said, accusingly.

"That you got shot?"

"That I'm stuck here in this bed," Roper said. "The least those bastards could have done was shoot me in the front, so I could lie on my back. I *hate* lying on my stomach."

"Calm down, why don't you?" Clint asked, approaching the bed.

"How can I calm down?" Roper asked. "Do you know what this means? My getting shot?"

"Yes, I do," Clint said. "You've got a lot of enemies who'd like to see you dead."

"More than that," Roper said. "Somebody's panicking."

"About what?"

"About me looking into all these jobs."

"You think they got onto you?"

45

"That's what I think."

"How?"

"Somehow, that's all I know," Roper said. "I told you, Clint, there's somebody smart behind all of this."

"Well," Clint said, "you may be right about everything, but if you are, do you know what I think?"

"What?"

"If somebody is this smart, then they're too smart to fall for a phony trick like Idaho."

Roper started to speak but stopped as a spasm of pain hit him. He tensed and closed his eyes. When he opened them they seemed slightly out of focus to Clint.

"You're just trying to keep me from going," Roper finally said.

"I *would* try to keep you from going," Clint said, "but I really don't think we have to."

"Why not?"

Roper's eyes still look unfocused, and he seemed to be having trouble keeping them open.

"I'll tell you tomorrow," Clint said. "Get some rest and I'll see you in the morning."

"I'm getting out of here, tomorrow," Roper said. He was slurring his words and actually drifting off to sleep.

"Sure, Tal," Clint said. "See you tomorrow, my friend."

Clint left the room and paused just outside the door. He was pretty sure his idea was sound and that Roper, when he was completely awake, would go for it. That meant neither one of them was going to have to go to Idaho.

But that was just the good news.

As Clint left the hospital he recalled that the last time he was here Roper had been in this very hospital with another injury. He was starting to think that maybe he was bad luck for his friend.

As he passed the front desk a small man paused, waited until Clint had gone out, and then engaged the nurse—a nun—in conversation.

"I'm inquiring as to the condition of a friend of mine, Sister," William Halliday said. "I understand he was shot?"

"What's the name?"

"Roper, Talbot Roper."

She looked up the name and then said, "Oh, yes, here it is. Yes, he was shot, but he's doing well. The doctor does not think that he is in any immediate danger."

"So the wound was not serious?"

"It was serious," she said, with a professional smile, "but your friend should be all right. You don't have to worry."

Well," Bill Halliday said, with a sinking feeling in his stomach, "that's a relief, isn't it?"

Halliday left the hospital and knew that he should go directly to a telegraph office and send his employer a telegram informing him of what had happened. He did not quite have the nerve to do that, however. There was still time to set things right, especially with Roper now a stationary target.

He flagged down a passing horse-drawn cab and gave him the address of a saloon in a not very good part of the city.

Clint was halfway to his hotel when he remembered something else about the last time he was in Denver. Not only was Roper in the hospital, but there was an attempt made on his life while he was there. He had managed to rescue his friend alone that time, but this time they had to worry about two professional shooters. He was not at all sure he'd be able to do it alone, this time.

He altered his course and headed for the nearest police station. He was going to need the cooperation of a young policeman who he only knew by the name Roper had called him—Danny boy.

ELEVEN

By the time Clint got back to his hotel he felt better. He'd managed to locate the policeman he heard Roper call Danny boy. His name was Danny Gibson, and through him Clint got to the detective who was looking into the shooting. Through *him* Clint arranged for round-the-clock protection for Roper. That meant that Danny Gibson and four other policeman were going to be in and around the hospital all night. It would be very difficult for even two professionals to get by that many policemen in order to get to Talbot Roper.

Clint was a little surprised that he had gotten the protection he requested without argument, but apparently Roper had a good reputation with the police and that worked in his favor.

When Clint got to his room the scent of Ginger in the air was considerably stronger than it had been before. He found her sitting up in his bed, reading a book while she waited for him. He saw the author's name: Mark Twain. He didn't bother telling her that he was personally acquainted with Sam Clemens.

"Well, hello," she said, putting the book down. She was

wearing a nightgown which, while it covered her, fit her very closely and outlined her large breasts and protruding nipples. "How is he?"

"He going to be fine," Clint said. He took the Colt New Line from his belt and put it on the night table. He looked at the gun belt hanging on the bedpost and knew he'd be wearing that from now on.

"You were gone so long I was beginning to worry."

"I was halfway back here when something occurred to me." He explained about arranging protection for Roper.

"He's lucky to have a friend like you."

"I don't know about that." He sat on the bed and started to remove his boots. "He got hurt the last time I was here, too. Maybe I'm a jinx."

She got to her knees and put her arms around him from behind. Her breasts were pressed tightly into his back.

"I don't believe in jinxes," she said. "I think it's in the nature of his work for him to get hurt once in a while."

"You're probably right."

"Are you tired?"

"Yes."

"Too tired?"

"What did you have in mind?"

"Something that would relieve stress," she said, sliding her hand into his shirt from behind, "but wouldn't necessarily be relaxing—at least, not right in the beginning."

"Sounds promising."

She unbuttoned his shirt so she could put both hands on his chest and whispered in his ear, "It is."

It was later, the second time they were having sex that night. Clint was crouched between Ginger's widespread legs, his cock buried deep inside of her, her strong legs wrapped around him, his hands beneath her, cupping her ass and pulling her too him every time he drove himself into her. Suddenly the door to the room was kicked open. The only thing that saved them was that the men who kicked it in did not know that the room was a two-room suite.

Clint heard the door and immediately disengaged himself from Ginger. As he reached for his gun with one hand, plucking it from the holster on the bedpost, he pushed her off the bed with the other, to the safety of the floor.

Naked, he ran into the other room, where by the light of a lighted lamp he saw two men standing in the doorway, looking confused. They saw him at the same time, but they were not as quick. He shot them both before they had time to bring their guns to bear. One of them went down right there, the other backpedaled into the hall and fell dead out there.

"Wha-what happened?" Ginger asked, coming up behind Clint. She pressed herself to him, and even though he had just killed two men he was aware of her breasts and her pubic bush rubbing against him.

"Let's get some clothes on," he said. "Looks like we're going to have some company."

TWELVE

First the management of the hotel arrived, full of apologies for letting such a thing happen. After that the police came, and Clint gave them the name of the detective who was working on the Roper shooting. After that it was just a matter of waiting for him to arrive. Meanwhile, the bodies were removed and one policeman waited with Clint and Ginger, who had both gotten dressed. However, while Clint had put on his shirt and Levi's, Ginger had only put on her nightgown, and the young policeman could not keep from stealing glances at her.

Finally, she said, "I'm going to wait in the bedroom."

"I don't think the detective will have to talk to you," Clint said. "Why don't you go to sleep?"

"Who can sleep?"

When the detective arrived he sent the young policeman down to the bar for a bottle of whiskey.

"Sir?" the younger man said.

"Whiskey," Detective Liam Donovan said. "You know what whiskey is, don't you, boy?"

"Yessir."

"Come back with a bottle."

53

"Uh, and glasses, sir?"

Donovan looked at Clint.

"I have glasses."

"Just the bottle, lad," Donovan said, "and be quick about it."

"Yessir."

After the policeman left, Donovan looked at Clint and said, "Two shootings in one day make me thirsty. Could you use a drink, then?"

"I could, yes.

"Good. While we're waiting for the bottle maybe you can tell me what happened here."

Clint did, and Donovan listened intently, then laughed quietly when Clint finished.

"What's funny?"

"Those poor lads had probably never been in a fancy hotel like the Denver House," Donovan said. "It probably never occurred to them that you wouldn't be right there in front of them when they kicked the door in."

"Well," Clint said, and he had to smile, "they did have surprised looks on their faces."

"I don't wonder," Donovan said. He looked at the door and said, "I wonder where that lad is with the bottle."

He turned back to Clint.

"You'll be thinkin' this has somethin' to do with the Roper shooting. Am I right, sir?"

"Yes, you are."

"Doesn't figure."

"Why not?"

"The men who tried for Roper were professionals," Donovan said. "These men were obviously just hired guns."

"Somebody thought I'd be easier than Roper," Clint said.

"Lucky for you they were wrong."

There was a knock on the door.

"Ah, that would be the lad."

Donovan opened the door and happily accepted the bottle from the young policeman.

"That'll be all then, lad," he said. "You can go home."

"Yes, sir."

"Yer a fine boy."

"Uh, thank you, si—" But the man was cut off when Donovan slammed the door.

He turned to Clint and asked, "Have you got those glasses, then?"

"Coming up."

Over a few drinks Clint and Donovan discussed the situation. Clint noticed that the detective thoroughly enjoyed his whiskey, actually smacking his lips several times after a sip.

"So tell me, then," he said, pouring himself a third glass, which Clint refused. He was still working on his second and it was all he was going to have. No point in getting drunk since there was no way of knowing if this would be the only attempt on his life for the night. "Why couldn't this just be somebody who recognized you and knew your reputation?"

"That would be coincidence."

"And?"

"I don't believe in coincidence."

"Well, maybe you don't believe in them, or like them, but they do happen," Donovan said. "I run into them all the time, in my business."

"Well, not this time."

"You're convinced?"

"Yes."

"All right, then." Donovan set aside the glass of whiskey he had been working on, folded his arms across his chest, and looked at Clint.

"Convince me."

THIRTEEN

Clint wasn't sure how Roper would react to what he was doing, but he told Detective Donovan what they were working on and what they had planned—until Roper was shot.

"I would have thought that a man like Talbot Roper was kept pretty busy," Donovan said.

"He is, as far as I know."

"Then why would he be involved in some . . . some fantasy about robberies being connected and planned by some unknown mastermind?" Donovan asked "I mean, doesn't any of that sound like coincidence to you, Mr. Adams?"

"Not the way Roper explained it to me."

"So you buy into his fantasy completely?"

"What makes you think it's a fantasy?"

"Well, just like you don't believe in coincidence," Donovan said, "I guess I don't believe in criminal masterminds."

He stood up, took one last look at the whiskey bottle, then turned and started for the door.

"Here," Clint said, grabbing the bottle and following

him. "Take this with you. I won't be needing it."

Donovan turned, looked at the bottle, and then grabbed it.

"Thanks."

"What about tonight?"

"Both men are dead," Donovan said, "and we have no idea if they came after you on their own or if they were sent."

"They were sent."

"That's what you say," Donovan said. "I let you talk me into putting five men on Roper at the hospital. That wasn't hard, actually, because he *was* bushwhacked. Do you want me to station some men in the hotel?"

"No, that won't be necessary."

"And what about the lady?" Donovan asked. "Would you like someone to escort her home?"

"No," Clint said, "she'll be staying with me. She'll be safe."

"That's what I thought." He opened the door. "Looks like it will still lock. Lucky."

"Yeah."

"I'll check back with you again tomorrow to see if we—or you—have found out something."

"That's fine."

He started out the door, then turned and asked, "This kind of thing *has* happened to you before, hasn't it, Mr. Adams?"

"It has, Detective."

Donovan nodded and said, "That's what I thought. Good night, sir."

"Good night."

He closed the door after Donovan and then walked into the bedroom. Ginger had not gone to sleep. Instead she was sitting up reading her book again. When he entered she put it down in her lap.

"What happened?"

"Nothing."

"What are they going to do about this?"

"Nothing."

"What?"

Clint explained to her how he tried to explain to the detective how this was connected with the attempt on Roper's life earlier in the afternoon.

"And he didn't believe you?"

"No. He thinks it was a coincidence. He thinks this is just another case of somebody trying to make a name for themselves"

"And could it have been that?"

"It could," Clint said, "but it's not."

She put her book aside and once again wrapped her arms around him from behind.

"Come to bed."

"I want to stay alert," he said, "so I don't think we should—"

"I just meant come to bed to sleep," she added, cutting him off, "that's all."

He got in bed with her, under the sheet, made sure his gun was in the holster hanging on the bedpost, and then turned down the lamp.

"You are going to sleep, aren't you?" she asked.

"I'll do my best."

"Do you want me to stand watch?" she asked.

"No," he said, running his hand up and down her arm, "you go to sleep, Ginger. In the morning I'll see you safely home."

"Not until you buy me a great big breakfast, though."

"That'll make up for almost getting you killed?" he asked.

She laughed softly and said, "It will be a start."

FOURTEEN

As promised Clint took Ginger down to the hotel dining room and bought her a big breakfast. He had one right along with her—steak and eggs and everything else they could get with it.

"Almost getting killed gives you an appetite," she said. "If this happens to you a lot I'm surprised you aren't fat."

"It happens," he said, "but not every day."

"What are you going to do today?"

"I'm going to go and see Tal," he said. "We still have some talking to do about his plan."

"He can't go through with it now, can he?" she asked. "Whatever it is?"

"That's what we're going to talk about."

After breakfast she insisted that she didn't need an escort all the way home.

"After all," she said, "nobody's after me."

"You have a point," he said. "All right, I'll put you in a cab and send you home."

"Not till I finish my breakfast, you won't!"

Clint poured himself another cup of coffee, sat back

and watched the lady eat. He'd seen very few women who'd be able to stay with her when it came to putting away food.

When she was finished he paid the bill and walked her to the front door and asked the doorman to get her a cab.

"I'll come by tonight to see what's going on," she said, and then was running to the cab before he could ask her where she lived. He had no idea how to get in touch with her.

He had the doorman get another cab, and he took this one to the hospital.

He had to identify himself to the policeman in the lobby of the hospital before the man would let him in to see Roper. When he entered the room Roper was lying on his left side, facing away from the door.

"Tal?"

"Clint? Come around where I can see you."

He walked around to the other side of the bed and stood where Roper could see him. The man's pallor was better, not as pale as the night before.

"Got tired of lying on my stomach," Roper said. "This is better, but I can't get them to turn the bed around so that my back is not to the door."

"This might be better, Tal," Clint said. "There are policemen in the hall. I don't know if you'd want your back to the window."

"You might have a point," Roper said. "Can you get me a gun? I feel like a sitting duck, here."

Clint was wearing his gun belt, but he had anticipated his friend's request. He took the Colt New Line from his belt and handed it to Roper, who tucked it away under his pillow.

"Thanks," he said. "This'll have to do until you can get me my gun or something bigger."

"I'll work on it. How do you feel?"

"Like getting out of this bed and out of this hospital," Roper said. "We've got to get to Idaho tomorrow. I've got a meeting set with some people—"

"Do you remember anything we talked about yesterday?"

"Last night?" Roper frowned. "It's all kind of blurry. What did we talk about?"

"I told you I had thought of another plan," Clint said. "One where we wouldn't have to go to Idaho."

"I don't remember that," Roper said. "Did I agree?"

"I didn't outline it," Clint said. "You were sort of fading in and out on me. I thought I'd just let you sleep and come back to discuss it today."

"Well, let's discuss it now, then," Roper said. "After all, I'm pretty much a captive audience."

Clint looked around, snagged a chair, and pulled it over to the bed.

"I was thinking about what you said about the man behind all this," Clint said. "About how smart you think he is."

"So?"

"I think he'd be too smart to fall for a phony stunt like a phony payroll in Idaho," Clint said.

"What are you suggesting, then?"

"With all the research you've done," Clint said, "on all the jobs that have been pulled, don't you think you could predict where he might hit next?"

"You mean an actual payroll or shipment of some kind?" Roper said. "Instead of some phony piece of bait?"

"Exactly."

"I could do that, I suppose," Roper said, "but there's bound to be several of them around the country."

"If you could narrow it down to two or three," Clint

said, "depending on where they are I'm sure I could get us some help."

Roper eyed Clint suspiciously.

"Is this your way of keeping me immobile for a while?"

"It's one way," Clint said, "but it's still a good idea, don't you think?"

"Actually, I do," Roper said. "I don't know why I didn't think of it. It does reduce the amount of planning and work my plan would have entailed."

"Okay, then," Clint said. "I can bring you whatever you need and you can do the research from here. In fact, we can both do it."

Roper shifted in the bed, trying to get more comfortable, and said, "I'll give it another day here, but then I'm going home. I can do the research from there, too. Deal?"

Clint smiled, and said, "Deal."

FIFTEEN

Clint brought Roper all the newspapers he could covering the past month. For the kind of booty they needed there would have to be a major story somewhere.

"You know what I'm thinking?" Clint asked, later in the day. His fingers were black from the newsprint and there was a smudge of it on his face.

"What?" Roper was eating from a hospital tray, which he had in his lap. He was sitting up, with several pillows propped behind him. It was a position he hadn't dared try before, but he needed to be right to do the research. Now he found that using the proper care, he could sit this way and even lean back, as long as he avoided pressure on his wound.

"Anybody shipping or holding something valuable enough for our purposes," Clint said, "would not let it appear in the newspaper."

"This guy would have a network," Roper said. "He'd manage to find out about it, anyway."

"Then how do we find out?" Clint asked.

"I've got a network," Roper said. "I'll put out the word—you'll have to send some telegrams for me."

"No problem."

"Hey, what about your friend Hartman?" Roper asked, suddenly. "He's got a hell of a network, hasn't he?"

"Jesus, I forgot," Clint said. "I sent him a telegram already. I wonder if the hotel clerk is holding a reply."

"Why don't you go and find out?" Roper said. "Leave me here with all these newspapers. Get me a piece of paper and a pencil and I'll give you some telegrams to send."

"All right," Clint said, looking down at his hands. "It'll be nice to wash this ink off my hands." He headed for the door.

"And see if you can get one of the sisters to bring me some coffee."

Once he had Roper set up with all the newspapers and some coffee, he left with his friend's telegrams in his pocket. He'd go to the Denver House first and see if they had a reply for him from Rick Hartman. Then he'd go to the telegraph office and send off Roper's telegrams and some of his own. They were going to need some help on this and he needed to find out who he could find and who he could count on.

When he entered the lobby of the hotel he went directly to the front desk.

"Do you have any telegrams for me?" he asked the clerk.

"One second, Mr. Adams." The man turned and checked all the mail cubbyholes. "Yes, sir, we have one. It came yesterday, but in all the excitement—"

"That's okay," Clint said. "No need to apologize. Just give it here."

"Yes, sir." The clerk handed it over. "Sir, the manager wanted me to ask you if you wanted your room changed?"

"No, it's fine. The lock on the door still works."

"Very good, sir," the man said. "I'll tell him."

"Fine." He wanted to get away from the clerk so he could read the telegram. He walked away, sat on one of the lobby divans and opened the envelope. It was from Hartman, who said he knew nothing of the kind of man or gang Clint was asking about, but he would continue to check further. That was fine. Clint hadn't expected Rick to come up with something immediately. He put the telegram back in the envelope and stuck it in his pocket. Time to go to the telegraph office and send out some of his own. As he stood, though, he saw Detective Donovan enter the hotel. The man started for the desk, but then spotted Clint and altered his course.

"Mr. Adams," the detective said. "On your way out?"

"Actually, I was," Clint said.

"Do you have a minute?" Donovan asked. "I thought you might like to know who your friends from last night were."

"I have a few minutes for that," Clint said.

Donovan looked past Clint to the entrance to the hotel bar and said, "I'm kind of dry."

Obviously, the man wanted more than a few minutes.

"Why not let me buy you a drink?" Clint asked.

Donovan's face lit up and he said, "What a kind offer. I accept."

SIXTEEN

Donovan didn't speak again until they were at a table, he with an Irish whiskey and Clint with a beer.

"I thank you for this," he said, sipping the whiskey and smacking his lips. "Tracking down murderers is dry work."

"Murderers?"

"Well," Donovan said, "that's what we found out. The two men you killed were hired killers, themselves. They've been wanted for some time in connection with some other killings in our fair city. So you see, you've gone and done us a favor without even realizin' it."

"If that's a thank-you," Clint said, "you're welcome, except that I don't consider killing anyone a favor."

"Well, ya did, though, didn't ya?" Clint had a feeling this wasn't Donovan's first drink of the day, and as he drank this one, his Irish accent seemed to grow thicker. "And they didn't leave ya much choice, did they?"

"No, they didn't. What about the shooting at Roper's office?"

"Ah," Donovan said, "nobody saw nothin', or if they did they ain't talkin', are they? Is he still in the hospital, then?"

"Yes, and I'd appreciate you leaving your men there one more night," Clint said. "He'll probably be going home tomorrow."

"And will you be wantin' us to provide protection while he's home, then?" Donovan asked.

"No," Clint said, "I'm sure once he's home we can handle it from there."

"Good." Donovan finished his drink and stood up. "Well, you were on your way out and I won't be keepin' you any longer. T'anks for the drink."

The two men shook hands.

"I'll walk you out," Clint said.

"No need," Donovan said. "I'm just goin' over there to the bar to buy meself another one. I'll be in touch, though."

"All right," Clint said. He left, wondering if Donovan would ever make it out of the bar.

At the telegraph office he sent off four telegrams from Roper and then three for himself. He told the clerk to send all replies to him at the Denver House Hotel.

"Even Mr. Roper's?"

"Yes," Clint said, "even those."

He left the telegraph office, which was walking distance from the hotel, and started back to the hotel. After a couple of blocks he had the feeling he was being followed. He wasn't sure, though, so he decided to test it out. He took an entirely illogical route back to his hotel, walking up one block and down another, stopping to look in windows and using the windows to look behind him. He finally came to the conclusion that there was someone following him, but he could never get a good look at them, so he decided to take a more definite approach to finding out.

He was going to ask them.

• • •

Three blocks from his hotel was a saloon called Morely's. He'd stopped in there once or twice during his travels, but not often enough to be recognized. He decided to go inside and have a drink and see what happened. If his tail followed him in then he'd be able to brace them right at the bar. If not, he'd try something else.

As it turned out he sat down at a table by the window, which he never did. It made him too good a target for someone from a rooftop or doorway across the street, but he didn't intend to be there long. He sipped the beer and peered out at the street from between the "R" and the "E" in Morely's. Sure enough his tail was in a doorway across the street, showing no signs of coming in. Clint left his beer on the table and went to the bar.

"Is there a back door?" he asked the bartender, a big burly man with a heavy beard.

"There is," the man said, "but it ain't for customers."

Clint put a dollar gold piece on the bar and asked, "How about just this one time?"

The man grabbed the dollar and said, "Right through that curtained doorway in the back."

"Thanks."

Clint went through the door, which led to a hallway. He took that until he reached the back door and stepped outside. He was behind the saloon, now, where they kept their garbage. The stench was overpowering and there were flies all around. He made a mental note never to eat there.

He found an alley that led to the street and peered out from it to see if his tail was still there. He was. All he could make out was a shadowy figure in a doorway. Hopefully, whoever it was wouldn't look down the block, but would keep their eyes on the front door of the saloon. Clint had to get across the street and would then move from doorway to doorway until he reached the one he wanted. He just needed to make it across right now without being seen.

He couldn't see the tail now. He had withdrawn deep into the doorway. It was time to move. He left the alley and walked across the street. He didn't want to run, because that might attract attention.

He made it to the other side and found safe haven in a doorway. He waited, then peered out. He saw no one, so moved to the next doorway, and then the next, and then the next . . .

Eventually, he was in the doorway next to the one his tail was in. There was no way to escape now, so he simply stepped out of his doorway and went to the other one—and found it empty.

He looked around, but saw no one. There were two options. Either he went through the door or he'd crossed the street and entered the saloon, Morely's.

The door was unmarked and solid. Clint tried it and found it locked. Of course, the tail could have locked it from the inside, but he would have had to get it open first. Clint tried to force it, but it held. It could have been unlocked, though, when the tail stepped in the doorway.

He had no choice. He had to go and check Morely's again. He crossed the street and entered, looked around, but he didn't know who he was looking for. It could have been anyone.

He walked to the bar and the bartender looked at him in surprise.

"You playin' some kind of game?"

"No game," Clint said. He put another dollar on the bar and it disappeared.

"Want to use the back door again?"

"Just information."

"About what?"

"Did anyone come in after I went out the back?"

"No."

"Are you sure?"

"I'm positive."

Clint cursed inwardly. Whoever had been following him was apparently good at what he did. Maybe he'd wanted Clint to see him, and when Clint started going through his elaborate plan to sneak up on him, he managed to disappear.

"Thanks," he said to the bartender.

"Hey," the man said, putting the dollar in his pocket to join the other one, "anytime."

Clint went outside and stood in the doorway of the saloon. He looked around. Was his tail watching him from somewhere, laughing? Was it someone who worked for the man Roper was looking for, the man Donovan did not believe was a criminal mastermind of some kind?

He left the doorway and started walking to his hotel. He checked behind him once or twice, but could not detect a tail. Maybe he was there and just didn't want to be seen, this time.

On the trail Clint wouldn't have thought someone could tail him without his knowing it. On a city street like this, though, he didn't claim to be as good as he was on the trail. If he was dealing with someone who lived in this city, they were definitely going to have the upper hand.

In some areas.

SEVENTEEN

Clint had dinner alone at the hotel. He figured to go to the hospital afterward, despite the fact that visiting hours would be over. He knew the police on duty would let him go to Roper's room. He'd check with the desk before he left to see if he'd gotten any replies to the telegrams he sent, but he didn't really expect any before morning.

He assumed that Roper would be going home in the morning, but they were going to have to discuss whether or not his friend would actually go home, or if they should put him somewhere else for a while—at least until he got back on his feet.

There was one other thing Clint was going to do when he saw Roper. He was going to try to talk him out of going after this "mastermind" he thought he had discovered. If he couldn't talk him out of it, maybe he could convince him to put it off for a while. Of course, that would probably depend a lot on who Roper's client was in this matter. Roper took his responsibilities very seriously, and if he felt a responsibility to this client he'd finish the job even if he had to do it crawling.

Clint wondered again who the client was, and why it was such a secret?

Over dinner he thought again about the tail. Had it been his imagination? He doubted it. He did actually see someone in the doorway across from the saloon. Somehow, whoever it was had gotten away, and if he was still following Clint, he was keeping well hidden.

Was everything connected? The attempt on Roper, the attempt on him, and then being followed? If they weren't then it was all coincidence, and that was something Clint didn't want to accept. He felt that not believing in coincidence had kept him alive more than once.

Over pie he wondered if Roper had found anything yet in all the newspapers he'd brought him? Or if they were going to have to depend on the answer to one of the telegrams.

He was finishing up his pie when he saw Detective Donovan enter the dining room and look around. He wondered why he wasn't surprised to see the man? It occurred to him that, over the years, he'd had lots of meals interrupted by conversations with lawmen. At least this one had waited until he was almost finished with dessert.

Donovan spotted him, smiled, waved, and came walking over like he was an old friend.

"Thought I might catch you here," Donovan said.

"Detective Donovan," Clint said. "Coffee?"

Donovan made a face, then said, "I suppose so. Thanks."

He sat down and a waiter appeared with a coffee cup, and filled it from the pot on the table.

"Thanks," Donovan said again, this time to the waiter.

"What can I do for you tonight, Detective?"

"I'm not sure, Mr. Adams," Donovan said. "I guess something's just eatin' at me a little."

"About what?"

"These shootings," Donovan said. "First Roper and

then you. I find myself in agreement with you, the more I think about it."

"Agreement with me?"

"About coincidence," the detective said. "Can't be a coincidence that you stop here in Denver to see your friend and then somebody tries to kill both of you."

Clint didn't comment.

"It must have something to do with what you're working on."

"The criminal mastermind?" Clint asked. "I thought you didn't believe in that?"

"Well, I'm still not convinced about that," Donovan said, "but somethin's goin' on, that's for sure."

"So what are you planning to do?"

"I don't know," Donovan said. He stared down at the coffee and pushed it away. "I know I'm not gonna drink that. Do you wanna go into the bar?"

"I have to stop by the hospital after this," Clint said.

"Oh, sure," Donovan said. "They gonna let Roper out tomorrow?"

"I think he's going to let himself out."

"And then what?"

"I don't know," Clint said. "I suppose he and I will talk about it tonight."

"It would seem risky to me for him to go home."

"Me, too."

"So if he didn't go home," Donovan asked, "where would he go?"

"I don't know."

"Here?"

"I can't say."

Clint wondered why the detective was suddenly concerned about where Roper was going to go.

"Well," Donovan said, getting to his feet, "I'll pull my men off the detail tomorrow morning, but you make sure

that you and Mr. Roper let me know if you need any more
help."

"We'll do that, Detective," Clint said. "I'm sure Roper
will be very grateful for the offer."

"Well," Donovan said, "watch your back."

"I always do."

Clint watched Donovan walk about and wondered what
was going on? Although the detective did not come all
the way around to Roper's way of thinking he had certainly come part way. Clint wondered why? Did Roper
have some friends who were higher up in the police de-
partment who might have put some pressure on the detective? Something else for him to ask his friend when he
saw him.

Still, that didn't explain Donovan's desire to know
where Roper would be staying when he left the hospital.
It occurred to Clint that wherever he and Roper decided
the man should stay, there should be only two people who
knew where it was—Clint and Roper, himself.

EIGHTEEN

"Fat Gator" Miller stared across his desk at Joe Pittman, digesting what the man had just told him.

"Let me get this straight," he said. "They shot Roper, but didn't kill him."

"Right."

"And then they went after Clint Adams?"

"Yes."

"Why?"

Pittman spread his hands helplessly.

"All I know is Roper and Adams were seen together. Our man there assumed they were working together and tried to get both of them."

"And got neither."

"Right."

Miller slammed his huge fist down on his desk. He was wearing a nightshirt, because it annoyed him to get dressed. He felt confined in regular clothes because of his bulk and chose to remain in a nightshirt whenever he was inside—which was most of the time.

"Unacceptable!" he snapped.

"Yes, sir."

"Do you see this desk?" he asked Pittman.

"Yes."

"You can't see the desk!" Miller yelled. "Do you know why?"

Pittman thought he did know why, but chose to say, "Uh, no, why?"

"Because it's covered with plans," Miller said. "How can I *make* plans for my next job when I know that the best detective in the country is out there looking for me? And now he may have help in the person of the Gunsmith?"

"It looks that way."

Miller sat back and his chair creaked, but held him.

"Wonderful."

"What?" Pittman was confused.

"I said it's wonderful."

"But . . . you just said it was unacceptable."

"No, no," Miller said, "you misunderstand . . . but it doesn't matter. What's wonderful is that I am not only going to outsmart the best detective in the country, but one of the legends of the west, as well." He sat forward again, the chair creaking dangerously. "I don't want any more attempts on their lives, do you understand?"

"Um . . . yes?"

"It will be better for me to pull the next job right under their noses than to kill them," Miller said. "Much, much better."

"Um, okay."

"Send the appropriate telegram," Miller said. "Remember, no further attempts on their lives."

"I understand."

"Then go do it!"

Pittman turned and rushed from the room.

Fat Gator looked down at his desk. He hadn't chosen his next job yet, but it was going to be a big one. And given his adversaries, the biggest one yet.

NINETEEN

When he entered Roper's hospital room he was glad to see his friend sitting up and looking wide-eyed and awake.

"I've got it narrowed down to three," he said, excitedly.

"If he picks the way we're picking," Clint said.

"Well, yeah," Roper said. "Come and look."

A gold shipment, a payroll, and a diamond shipment. New Mexico, California, and Missouri."

"Diamonds?" Clint asked. "In Missouri?"

"They're being taken up and down the Mississippi on display," Roper said. "It's not so much a shipment as a show."

"A show?"

"Hey," Roper said, "people like to look at diamonds. What can I tell you?"

"Probably women, mostly."

"Whatever. What's important is that they're valued at a hundred thousand dollars."

Clint whistled.

"Why would anyone want to put diamonds that valuable on a riverboat on the Mississippi?"

"That's something else I don't care about," Roper said.

They discussed the diamond shipment some more, and the other two jobs. The others made more sense, because they didn't involve water. In both cases all somebody'd need was some good horses.

"I vote for the payroll," Clint said.

"Why?"

"Easier to transport than gold," Clint explained, "and easier to spend than diamonds."

"You may have a point," Roper said, "but I think our man would be intrigued by the whole diamond thing."

"Take it as a challenge, you mean?"

"Right."

"Well then, *you* may be right," Clint conceded.

"What about those telegrams?"

"They all went out," Clint said, "but nothing came back, yet."

"And Hartman?"

Clint explained that he'd heard from Rick, but he'd had no info. He was going to keep looking. He also told Roper that he sent some telegrams to some friends to see who would be available to help.

"Good," Roper said. "Now all we need to find out is where we're going to need the help."

"Can we talk about something else?"

"What?"

"You leaving the hospital."

Roper held up his hand.

"I'm not staying here another day."

"I said that wrong," Clint said. "I want to talk about where you're going to stay when you leave."

"I'm ahead of you," Roper said. "I don't want to be home. It would be too easy for them to try again."

"Exactly."

"I know of a couple safe houses," Roper said. "They're hotels in a part of town people don't usually go to."

"Sounds great."

"It is," Roper said. "I know the owners, and the security would be good."

"Speaking of which," Clint said, "you must be friends with Donovan."

"The detective? No, I just met him," Roper said. "Why?"

"He's very anxious to be of help," Clint said. "He asked me where you were going to be staying once you left here."

"Why should he care?"

"That's what I want to know," Clint said. "You have some friends in high places?"

"A few, maybe," Roper said, "but nobody who'd put any pressure on him."

"Makes it even more odd, doesn't it?" Clint asked.

"What about his men?"

"He's pulling them off tomorrow."

"That's fine," Roper said. "We won't need them after tomorrow."

They went over some of the jobs in the newspaper again and again they decided to agree on the three Roper had settled on before Clint arrived.

"Depending on what replies we get from our telegrams," Roper said, "we'll just have to go with these three and see what happens."

"All right," Clint said, in agreement, "then let's get rid of all this other stuff so it's not in the way."

He collected all the newspapers Roper had spread out on the bed, crumpled them up, and deposited them in a corner.

"How are you feeling?" Clint asked.

"It only hurts when I think about it," Roper said. "Like when somebody asks me about it."

"Sorry."

"Forget it," Roper said. "How'd you get them to let you in here, anyway? It's after visiting hours."

"Your friend Danny boy is out there."

"There's a kid who's ambitious," Roper said. "He might be my friend in high places someday."

"Then maybe he'd like to help now?"

"Sure he would. What did you have in mind?"

"Maybe," Clint said, "some questions about our new friend, Detective Donovan."

TWENTY

They hadn't discussed whether or not Ginger was going to come by that night, but Clint found himself a little disappointed she wasn't there when he got back to his hotel. The maid has changed the sheets on the bed again— he was going to have to tell her to stop doing that—so there was no hint of Ginger's scent in the bed when he went to sleep.

In the morning he arrived at the hospital with a cab to pick up Roper. The detective was ready, sitting in a wheelchair in the lobby with the policeman Danny standing next to him. He was not in uniform. The other men who had been on the detail had already left.

Clint entered the lobby and shook hands with Danny.

"Mr. Roper said you wanted to talk to me?" he asked.

"Can you ride with us, Danny?" Clint asked. "Roper said it would be all right if you knew where he was staying."

"Danny's a good kid, Clint," Roper said. "We can trust him."

Danny stood straight up and said, "I'd be honored to ride with you."

"Good," Clint said, "you can help me get his butt into the cab."

They pulled up in front of one of the hotels Roper had talked about in a run-down section of Denver. Clint had not yet approached the young officer with the subject he wanted to discuss.

They got out of the cab and helped Roper down. Clint paid the driver and they went inside. They were immediately accosted by a big man with broad shoulders and an even broader smile.

"My friend Roper!" he shouted.

He seemed about to grab Roper in a bear hug and Clint quickly stepped between them.

"I'm afraid a hug would kill him, right now," Clint said, holding his hands up. "No offense."

"You are injured?" the man asked. He had an accent that was unknown to Clint.

"I was shot two days ago, Dimitri," Roper said. "I need a place to lay low for a while."

"And you picked my humble hotel?" Dimitri asked. "I am honored. I will give you the best room in the house."

Clint looked around and figured that would be the room with the least dust and bugs in it.

"Dimitri, these are my friends, Danny and Clint. Along with you they are the only ones who know I'm here."

"And we will keep it that way, my friend," Dimitri said. "I assure you."

"Clint, Danny, this is Dimitri Cosmocropoulas."

"Cosmo—?" Danny tried but stopped there.

"Just call me Dimitri. You are not shot?" he asked Danny and Clint.

"No," Clint said.

"Then Dimitri hugs you!" the big man said, and did so.

He grabbed them each in a bear hug that lifted them both off their feet, in turn.

"And now I take you to your room!" Dimitri announced. Every line he spoke sounded like either an announcement or an exclamation.

"Top floor would be preferable, Dimitri," Roper said. "Something without easy access from outside."

"Top floor it is, then," Dimitri said. "Come. I get your key."

He went behind the front desk and grabbed a key, then came around, bidding them, "Come, come," until they followed him up the stairs, moving at Roper's pace.

They followed down a hall on the second floor until he stopped at a door, fit the key in, and opened it.

"There! Best room in the house. One window looks over the alley in the back. No ledge, no roof. No access from the window."

Clint walked to the window and looked out, saw that Dimitri was correct. It was a sheer drop to the ground below.

"Looks good," he said to Roper.

Clint looked around and was surprised to see that everything was not covered in dust.

"I keep my rooms clean," Dimitri said, noticing Clint's gaze.

"I didn't mean—"

"Is all right," Dimitri said, waving off any apology. "Everyone want drinks? I bring up cold beer."

"Not for m—" Danny started, but was interrupted.

"Cold beer sounds good, Dimitri," Roper said. "Thanks."

"I be back."

Dimitri left and closed the door behind him, leaving the three of them there alone.

"He's a character," Clint said.

"Came here from Greece about ten years ago," Roper said.

"How'd you meet him?"

"During one of my cases," Roper said. "I helped him and his family out of a bad jam. He feels he owes me."

"So we can trust him?"

"Absolutely," Roper said. "He takes his debt very seriously."

"That's good," Clint said.

Roper went over and sat on the bed.

"Why don't you tell our young friend here what you want from him, Clint?" he suggested. "He's about to bust from curiosity."

Clint turned and looked at Danny, who looked back at him, expectantly.

"There's something only you can help us with, Danny," Clint said.

Danny didn't respond. He didn't ask what it was. He just waited.

TWENTY-ONE

"You want me to what?"

"Get us as much information as you can on Detective Donovan."

Danny looked at Roper.

"Is he serious?"

"I'm afraid he is."

"But . . . why? Why do you want me to spy on a fellow officer?"

"We don't want you to spy, Danny," Clint said. "We need to know if we can trust Donovan as much as, say, we trust you. Before we can do that we need to find out as much as we can about him. You can understand that, can't you?"

"Well . . . I guess."

"Danny," Roper said.

The young policeman looked at the private detective.

"I don't want you to do anything you don't feel comfortable doing," Roper said. "Tell us to go to hell and I'll understand."

"I wouldn't want to do that, Mr. Roper."

"Well then, tell us no, or tell us you'll think about it.

Whatever you want to tell us is fine with me."

Danny stared at Roper for a few moments, then looked at Clint.

"Me, too," Clint said, "if that matters."

Before the young officer could answer someone kicked at the door. When Clint opened it Dimitri came in carrying a tray with four beer mugs on it.

"Here we go," Dimitri said. "Cold beers for everyone to celebrate my friend Roper coming to stay in my hotel."

He held the tray out while Clint and Danny each took a beer, then carried it over to Roper so he could have his. He took his last.

"To my friend!" he said, and drank his down while the others had some of theirs. Clint and Roper drank half while Danny just sipped.

"Oh," Dimitri said, "by the way, this room is ten dollars a week."

"Ten dollars?" Clint asked. "You're going to charge your friend—"

"Ten dollars is fine, Dimitri," Roper said. "And thanks for the beer."

"Just leave the mugs," Dimitri said. "I pick them up later."

"Thanks, Dimitri."

Dimitri left and Clint looked at Roper.

"He owes you so much and he's going to charge you for the room?" he demanded.

"And for the beer, you can bet," Roper said, laughing. "Relax, Clint, I knew he'd charge me. After all, this hotel is his business."

"But not his only business," Danny said.

"What?" Clint asked.

"Danny's a policeman," Roper said. "He knows that Dimitri has other, uh, ways to make money . . . but we don't have to talk about that, do we, Danny?"

"No, sir," Danny said, "not if you don't want to."

"Good."

Danny put his beer mug down on a chest of drawers nearby.

"About that other thing."

"Yes?" Roper asked.

"I have always sort of wondered about Detective Donovan myself," he said. "I guess maybe I could ask some questions, just to get some background."

"That's great, Danny," Roper said. "We'll need it in a day or two, and you can either come here and talk to me or go to Clint's hotel and discuss it with him."

"This is my hotel," Clint said.

"What?" Roper asked.

"As long as you're staying here, I might as well, too."

"You're going to give up the luxury of the Denver House for this place?" Roper asked.

"I am, and I'll go downstairs and see if I can get Dimitri's 'friend' rate of ten dollars a week."

"I'm sure he'll give it to you," Roper said. "Just remember to mention my name. He owes me, you know."

"So you told me," Clint said, and left to go downstairs.

TWENTY-TWO

Bill Halliday was confused. First Henry Miller wanted Roper killed and then he didn't. That meant that the two men who had been killed by Clint Adams had died for no reason.

Now all Halliday was supposed to do was keep tabs on Roper. Only problem with that was that by the time he got to the hospital, Roper had already left.

"That's odd," Halliday said to the nun who was at the front desk. "I was supposed to pick him up."

"Oh, dear," the middle-aged sister said, "but his other friend has already picked him up."

"Other friend?"

"Yes. Mr. Adams?"

"Oh, yes," Halliday said, "Mr. Adams. We must have gotten our signals crossed. He was supposed to pick him up if I couldn't."

"Well, I guess he misunderstood."

"I guess so," Halliday said. "Well, as long as he got picked up, everything is all right. Thank you, Sister."

He left the hospital. Somehow he doubted that Roper would go either home or back to his office, where he'd been shot. Chances were good the man would find a hole to crawl into, at least until his wound was healed. If only he knew that nobody was going to be taking any shots at him again.

Halliday decided that if he couldn't find Roper, he'd just have to find Adams and follow him. He left the hospital and went to the Denver House Hotel.

"He what?"

"I said Mr. Adams has checked out," the clerk repeated as if Halliday was hard of hearing.

"When?"

"Just a little while ago."

"Did he say where he was going?"

"No, he did not."

"Well, was he leaving town?"

"I'm afraid he didn't say, sir."

Halliday walked away from the desk without thanking the man. Apparently, he'd been a step behind both Roper and Adams today.

How was he going to explain that to his employer?

TWENTY-THREE

Clint moved into a room just next to Roper's. Since Dimitri's hotel—which was simply called the Greek Hotel—did not have a restaurant Clint brought Roper's meals into his room for him.

"Surely you can get someone to do this for us," Roper said, as Clint brought him his dinner the first night on a cloth-covered tray.

"That would be someone else who knew our whereabouts, Tal," Clint pointed out. "We don't want that."

"You have a point. Are you eating, as well?"

"No," Clint said, "this is all yours."

"It smells wonderful."

Clint pulled the cloth away to reveal a full steak dinner.

"Where did this come from?"

"Dimitri told me of a place a block away," Clint said. "He said it was owned by his cousin."

"That figures," Roper said.

"Enjoy your meal," Clint said. "I'll be back in a little while."

"Where are you going?"

"I didn't want to tell the Denver House where we were, which means I'll have to check with them occasionally for responses to our telegrams."

Roper cut a piece of steak, stuck it in his mouth, and said, "Get something to eat while you're out, too. I don't want you passing out from hunger on me."

"Don't worry," Clint said. "I always feed the inner beast."

"Bring back a bottle of whiskey too," Roper said, as Clint headed for the door. "You know, just for medicinal purposes."

"Yeah, right!"

Halliday decided to sit on the Denver House Hotel for a while, for want of something better to do. It was either that or try to come up with a telegram to his employer explaining how he had lost both Adams and Roper.

So he took a seat on a divan in the lobby and just waited.

Clint didn't go back to the Denver House right away. He'd only left there a couple of hours ago. He wanted to give it more time before he went back looking for telegrams.

He walked around a bit in the area where the Greek Hotel was, just to see if he was being followed. He couldn't detect anyone, but he already knew that didn't mean much. Still, he felt reasonably sure that he hadn't led anyone to the Greek Hotel, so Roper should be safe for a while.

He learned quickly that this was not an area the drivers liked bringing their cabs to, so he had to walk several blocks before he was able to flag one down.

"Where to?" the man asked.

That stumped him. Where to, indeed? Finally, he decided to go ahead and go to the Denver House. He could at least get something to eat someplace he knew had good food and then on the way out check in with the desk for telegrams.

He gave the man the location and sat back. He was going in circles, he knew, with no definite destination in mind. There was nothing to be done until they first agreed on a course of action, and then second, until Roper was sufficiently healed to *take* some sort of action. Also, they had to hear back from Danny about Detective Donovan. The man's questions about where Roper was going to be hiding out raised all kinds of red flags for Clint. The detective's job should have been finished once Roper left the hospital, and since they were not great friends, what was his motive for asking that question?

Hopefully, something Danny found out would supply the answer.

When Clint entered the lobby of the Denver House Hotel, Bill Halliday could not believe his luck. He admitted to himself then that he dared not leave the lobby of the hotel. It was fear that kept him there, and now his fear had brought him luck. He watched as Clint Adams entered the dining room, then went to the doorway to make sure he was being seated. He was obviously going to have a meal, and that gave Halliday time to make certain arrangements.

"We thought you'd left us for good, sir," the waiter said to Clint.

"Not quite for good," Clint said. "You still serve one of the best steaks in Denver."

"Yes, sir."

"Would you bring me a pot of coffee and let the desk clerk know I'm here in case something is left for me at the desk?"

"Yes, sir," the waiter said. "Right away."

When the waiter brought the coffee he brought three telegrams with him, all of which had been left at the desk within the past hour. Clint read them all over his first cup of coffee.

TWENTY-FOUR

It was halfway through his dinner that Clint saw Ginger enter the dining room. She saw him, waved, and came rushing over.

"What a coincidence," she said.

"Yes, isn't it?" he agreed.

"I asked for you at the desk but they said you checked out," she said. "May I sit with you?"

"Please."

She sat down and stared across at him all wide-eyed and cheerful.

"Were you trying to avoid me?"

"Why would I do that?" Clint asked.

"Why did you check out?"

"Business," he said. "I had to relocate."

"Oh, I see." She batted her eyes at him. "Would you be able to tell me where you're staying now?"

"I'm afraid not, Ginger."

She pouted.

"Why not?"

"I have some, uh, business partners who wouldn't like it."

"Business partners like who?"

He wagged his index finger at her. "They wouldn't like that, either."

She sat back in her chair and looked hurt. "Are you telling me I won't see you anymore?" she asked. "That we're . . . finished?"

"I'm afraid so."

She looked hurt. It was a great act, and if he hadn't know she was lying through her teeth, he might have felt bad.

"Well . . ." she said. "I don't know what to say."

"Say good-bye," he said. "Say it was fun, and see you around."

"Why are you doing this?"

"Because," he said, picking up his fork, "I don't believe in coincidence."

"Clint?"

"Good-bye, Ginger . . . if that's even your name."

She stared at him for a few moments, and then suddenly the expression on her face and her whole demeanor changed.

"Actually," she said, "it *was* fun while it lasted."

"Yes, it was."

"Too bad it had to end this way."

"I agree."

She stood up.

"You might not believe it right now," she said, "but we'll be seeing each other again."

He smiled up at her and said, "I'll hold my breath until then."

She smiled, shook her head, and said, "I underestimated you. It won't happen again."

He didn't say anything to that. She turned and walked out, her back straight, her head held high.

He wondered who the heck she really was.

• • •

Outside the hotel Halliday looked at her expectantly and said, "Well?"

"We've made a mistake."

"What mistake?"

"It doesn't matter," she said. She opened her purse, took out an envelope with money in it, and passed it to him. He grabbed it, but she didn't let go.

"Keep an eye on him," she said, warningly. "Don't lose him this time, do you understand?"

"I understand."

"And have someone cover the back," she said. "You don't have much time. He was almost finished eating."

"A-all right."

"Don't make any more mistakes, Halliday," she said. "They won't be tolerated any longer."

"Yes, all right."

She started to walk away.

"Where are you going?"

She just waved her hand at him over her shoulder without turning.

Now Clint was sure there was someone out in front of the hotel waiting for him to come out so they could follow him. He'd made a mistake in coming back here. He was sure Roper could have sent one of his street contacts to the hotel to pick up the telegrams. Doing it himself had been an unnecessary risk. He should have given it more thought, or talked it over with Roper.

He continued to eat, mulling over his next move. If they had someone out front they probably had someone in the back, too. As soon as he left the hotel he was going to have a tail on him.

He called the waiter over, ordered some more coffee, and a piece of peach pie. Whoever was waiting out there—front and back—he intended to see how much patience they had.

TWENTY-FIVE

Clint nursed a pot of coffee and a piece of pie as long as he could—then he ordered another of each. Just for variety, this time he ordered blueberry pie.

He wondered how many exits there were in a hotel this size. Had to be more than just two, front and back. When he finished the second pot of coffee and piece of pie, he paid his bill and then went out to the front desk.

"Did you get those telegrams, Mr. Adams?" the clerk asked.

"Yes, I did," Clint said. "Thank you."

"If any others come in we'll be glad to hold them for you."

"Thank you. That's very kind. There is something else you can do for me right now, though."

"Would you like your room back? It's still vacant."

"No, that's not it," Clint said. "How many ways out of this hotel are there?"

"Well," the clerk said, "there's the front and the back—"

"Any other ways?"

"Do you need another way?"

103

"Very much."

The clerk leaned on the desk and lowered his voice.

"Is it the police we're trying to avoid?"

"No," Clint said, also lowering his voice, "if it were the police I wouldn't be trying to avoid them."

"Ah, I see," the clerk said. "Well, there are other ways out of the hotel. Um, usually they're only used by employees, but I think we can make an exception in this case."

"I'd appreciate it."

"Which side of the building would you prefer to come out on?"

"That really doesn't matter," Clint said. "I didn't realize I'd have that much of a choice."

The clerk rang the bell for a bellhop and one appeared promptly.

"Front, would you show Mr. Adams the way to the freight entrance?"

"The freight entrance?" the boy asked.

"Yes," the clerk said, patiently, "that's the one we use for deliveries?"

"I know what the freight entrance is," the boy said, indignantly. "This way, sir."

"Thank you again," Clint said to the clerk, and followed the disgruntled bellhop into a section of the hotel usually reserved for employees.

"Thinks I don't know what the freight entrance is," the boy muttered as he led Clint through a maze of corridors.

"I guess you were just surprised that he wanted you to show it to me, huh?" Clint asked.

"Exactly," the boy said. "I was just surprised. I wasn't asking him what it was. He lords it over us just because he works the desk and we're bellhops."

"That's tough."

"Ain't so tough, actually," the boy said. "I wouldn't have his job if they gave it to me."

"Why's that?"

"We get tips, and he don't," the bellhop said. "He thinks he makes more money than we do, but when you figure in the tips, he don't."

"Guess he'd be upset to find that out, huh?"

"You bet he would. Here's the door, sir. Leaves you in an alley, if that's all right?"

"That's fine."

The bellhop opened the door and the sunlight streamed in. Clint took out a dollar and gave it to the boy.

"See what I mean?" the boy said, cheerfully. "Thanks."

"Thank you," Clint said. "This helps me out a lot."

"I hope they don't catch you."

Clint looked at him, then realized the boy thought he was trying to avoid the police.

"I don't think they will."

"I won't tell a soul you went out this way, sir."

"I appreciate it very much," Clint said. "Thanks."

He went out the door, and when it closed behind him, it locked automatically.

By using the alley he managed to avoid both the front and the rear of the hotel. By the time he got to the Greek Hotel he was certain he had not been followed. He had made a major mistake in going back to the Denver House Hotel, one he would not make again.

He entered the Greek and saw the Greek behind the desk.

"Ah, my new friend," Dimitri shouted. His voice was so loud Clint actually winced.

"Hello, Dimitri."

"And how is our mutual friend?"

"He was fine the last time I looked," Clint said. "I'm going to check on him now."

"And you?" Dimitri asked. "How do you like your room?"

"It's very clean." He started up the steps, but stopped when Dimitri continued to speak.

"And you expected something else?" Dimitri demanded. "I keep a very clean place."

"I can see that, Dimitri," Clint said.

"Not so nice, perhaps, as what you are used to," Dimitri said, "but clean. No one can say Dimitri Cosmocropoulas is not clean!" He pounded his chest to further bring home his point.

"I agree, Dimitri," Clint said. "No one can say that."

"Ha!" Dimitri said. "Go, then, and check on our wounded comrade. If he needs anything, you tell him to ask Dimitri."

"I will," Clint said. "I'll tell him."

When Dimitri did not speak again Clint felt it was safe to go up the stairs.

TWENTY-SIX

"The telegram from your twin," Miller said, "means they need you in Denver." He handed Pittman an envelope. "Here are your train tickets."

"When do I leave?"

"Tonight."

"One thing."

"What?"

"Why do you call us the twins?" Pittman asked. "We're not even related."

"Because," the former Fat Gator of Louisiana said, "you're the same on the inside."

"And how's that?"

"Dark."

Pittman frowned.

"Relax," Miller said. "It's a compliment, believe me."

"I'll need money."

"It's in the envelope."

"What about our next job?"

"You won't be far from it."

"You picked it out already?"

"Yes."

"What is it?"

"I'm not going to tell you, yet," Miller said. "You do what you've got to do in Denver, and then I'll let you know."

Pittman tapped the envelope against the palm of his left hand.

"Go, go, go," Miller said. "I don't want you to miss your train."

"I don't like operating this way," Pittman said.

Miller fixed him with a stern look.

"Would you rather operate the way you were when I found both of you?" he asked. "Rolling drunks, conning old ladies out of their savings? I've put money in your pockets, haven't I?"

"Yes, but—"

"Do either of you have a complaint about the way you live?"

"No, but—"

"Then why is there a 'but'?"

Pittman remained silent, then sighed and said, "There isn't. I'm on way to Denver."

"Good," Miller said. "Send me a telegram when you get there. I'll have instructions for you."

"Yes, sir."

"And don't worry," Miller said, "you're going to like what I have picked out for you. I guarantee it."

Pittman nodded and left. Miller sat back in his chair, ignored the shriek that came from it, plucked at the front of the nightshirt to air himself out beneath it, and then reached for a cigar and lit it.

Everyone was going to be surprised about the next job.

TWENTY-SEVEN

Clint told Roper about what had happened at the hotel.

"You say the girl's name was Ginger?" Roper asked.

"Yes," Clint said, "the girl you sent me the first night."

"Clint," Roper said, "the girl I sent you was named Gloria."

Clint stared at his friend.

"Are you sure?"

"Positive," Roper said. "I spoke to her early that day."

"But you asked me the next morning how I liked Ginger."

"I think I asked how you liked your present."

Clint thought a moment, then said, "I'll be damned, but I think you're right. Jesus, we could have saved some time if one of us had just said the girl's name."

"What's this woman look like?"

Clint described Ginger.

"Sounds good," Roper said, "but Gloria was a tall, slender blonde with real creamy skin and— Jesus, I wonder what happened to Gloria?"

"Take it easy," Clint said. "Maybe they just bought her off. After all, she is a working girl, right?"

"We have to check on her," Roper said, sitting up, putting his feet on the floor. "She's also a friend, Clint."

"Okay, but you sit tight," Clint said. "Can't we have Dimitri do it?"

"Yeah, as a matter of fact, he can," Roper said. "He might even know her. Dimitri knows a lot of the girls in Denver."

"Then I'll go down and ask him," Clint said. "After all, he wants to help, right?"

"Right."

"As long as you pay his bill."

"Lay off him about that, will you?" Roper asked. "He needs to make a living, doesn't he?"

"Sure he does," Clint said, and made a vow there and then not to mention it again. It seemed a sore spot with Roper. After all, these people—Dimitri, Gloria, and others like him—were his contacts and, apparently, his friends.

"So what do you think this Ginger wanted?"

"I don't know," Clint said. "She never made a move to do me any harm, but she was asking about you. Could be she's working with whoever shot at you and sent those two after me. Also, with whoever's been following me."

"And what about Donovan?" Roper asked. "What if they bought him off, as well as Gloria?"

"Whoever your criminal mastermind is," Clint said, "he's got to have some money."

"A lot of it," Roper said. "And it takes a lot of money to get a lot of money."

"You want to go over these telegrams?" Clint asked.

"Let me see them."

"Two from your contacts and one from one of the men I asked for help."

Roper took the telegrams and looked at them.

"My two don't seem to be much help," he said, putting them aside. "No information on any big money payrolls of bank deposits or gold deposits that haven't been covered by the newspapers."

He unfolded Clint's telegram and looked at it, then at Clint.

"Bat Masterson?"

"He's in Kansas, but is willing to hop a train and go anywhere we need him to," Clint said.

"Sometimes I'm amazed by who your friends are."

"You know what? So am I." He turned and headed for the door.

"Where are you off to?"

"I'll go and talk to your Greek friend about what happened to your other friend, Gloria."

"You might try describing Ginger to him, also," Roper suggested. "He might be able to put a name to the description."

"Good idea," Clint said. "I'll be back in a little while."

"Bring us bottle of whiskey!" Roper shouted as he went out the door. "You forgot this time!"

Clint went downstairs and found the good-natured Greek behind the desk, smiling as always.

"How is our friend?" he asked.

"He's fine," Clint said, "but he wanted me to ask you something."

"Ask!" Dimitri said, magnanimously. "Anything!"

"Do you know a girl named Gloria?" Clint asked. "A professional girl?"

"I knew Gloria very well." Suddenly, the Greek looked sad.

"Well, could you find out—wait a minute," Clint said, shaking his head as if trying to dispel a fog. "Did you say you *knew* her?"

"Yes," Dimitri said, "it was a great tragedy."

"What was?"

"Her death, of course."

"Dimitri," Clint said. "This is very important. How did she die?"

"She was murdered," Dimitri said. "Just a few nights ago. Her body was found in a vacant building not far from here."

"How was she murdered?"

"I heard she was strangled."

"I see," Clint said. "Well, thank you, Dimitri."

"But what was the question you wanted to ask?"

"That's all right," Clint said. "You've already answered it."

TWENTY-EIGHT

Clint wondered how Roper would react when he relayed the information to him about Gloria. Before he had a chance to go up, though, the young policeman, Danny Gibson, entered the lobby.

"Hey, Danny," Clint said. "Glad to see you."

"Yeah." Danny looked glum.

"What is it?" Clint asked. "What's wrong?"

"Can we go for a walk? We gotta talk."

"Sure, kid," Clint said. "Sure you don't want to go upstairs and talk to Roper?"

"Not yet," Danny said. "I want to talk to you, first."

"Sure," Clint said. At least this would keep him from having to give Roper the bad news, for a while. "Come on, let's walk."

Danny was not in uniform, so walking down the street in that neighborhood was not a problem. In fact, when they came to a saloon they stepped inside to get a drink and nobody even looked at them twice. They got a beer each and then sat down at a table near the back of the half-full place.

"What's on your mind?" Clint asked.

113

"I looked into Donovan's past, just like you asked."

"Already?"

"Well," Danny said, "it looks as if everyone knows about him but me. I feel so stupid."

"About what?"

"About not knowing what he was—is."

"Which is what?"

"A drunk," Danny said, "and, if what I hear is right—and it probably is—a dirty policeman."

"Ah . . ." Clint wondered if Danny had somehow idolized the detective, and was just now discovering the man's feet of clay.

"Everybody says he's on his way out, but he manages to hang onto his job."

"And how does he do that?"

"They say he's got a friend high up that keeps saving his ass," Danny said. "But everybody figures that sooner or later he's gonna do somethin' he can't be saved from."

"I'm sorry, kid," Clint said.

"It's just . . . disillusioning, is all," Danny said. "I mean, I want to be a detective somebody, but if he's an example of what detectives are like—"

"You don't have to be like that, Danny," Clint said, "just because he is. You're your own man. You can be anything you want. Be like Roper, only with a badge."

Danny rolled his eyes. "If I was as good a detective as Mr. Roper I wouldn't need to be a policeman."

"That's true," Clint said. "You could be whatever you wanted. A Pinkerton, maybe."

"Mr. Roper was a Pinkerton," Danny said, "but he and Allan Pinkerton couldn't get along."

"I know," Clint said, "and I know Allan, so I know why."

"Were you a Pinkerton?"

"No," Clint said, "I've just had dealings with the man. He's hard to work for, that's for sure."

"Well . . . what does this mean? I mean, as far as Mr. Roper is concerned?" Danny asked.

"I don't know. I suppose Donovan could have been trying to pump me for Roper's location because he's working for whoever shot him. Maybe he made sure he got assigned to the case so he could cover for whoever it was."

"That's probably true," Danny said. "It wasn't supposed to be his originally, but he got it, somehow."

"Calling on help from higher up, I guess."

Suddenly, Danny got a shocked look on his face.

"Jesus!"

"What?"

"What if whoever is helping him is also dirty? What if it's somebody real high up?"

The young man was really getting disillusioned, now.

"Don't jump to conclusions, Danny," Clint said. "Let's just deal with what we know."

"And what's that?"

"We know we don't want Donovan to know where we are."

Clint told Danny to go on about his job and they'd be in touch with him. He thanked him for the information. The young man walked back to the hotel with Clint, but did not want to stop in and see Roper. He just wasn't in the mood, and Clint couldn't much blame him.

"Before you go," Clint said, "what have you heard about the death of a prostitute named Gloria something?"

"All I know is that she was strangled, found in a vacant building," Danny said. "Why?"

"Just wondering."

"Is her death connected with what you're doing?"

"I don't know."

" 'Cause if it is," Danny said, "you should know that Detective Donovan has that case, too."

Clint stared at the young man for a few seconds, and then said, "Well now, that's very interesting."

"Do you want me to see what I can find out about it?"

"Sure," Clint said, "but discreetly, okay? We don't want Donovan to find out."

"I'll be real discreet," Danny said. "Don't worry."

Clint watched the young man rush off and wondered if he had ever been that young, or idealistic?

TWENTY-NINE

Clint finally went back up to Roper's room to tell his friend about Gloria's murder. He took it stoically and Clint waited for him to respond in his own time.

"It looks like I unwittingly put her in the middle of something and got her killed," he finally said.

"Tal—"

"No, it's okay," Roper said, putting up his hand. "Don't try to make me feel better by telling me it's not my fault. I know it's not. It's the fault of whoever killed her, and I'm going to make sure they pay."

"Meanwhile," Clint said, "Danny also came up with some information about Donovan which was interesting."

He relayed it all to Roper while the man listened silently.

"I hate lawmen who dishonor the badge," Roper said when Clint was finished.

"Well," Clint said, "I've met plenty of those over the years, and so have you. The question is, how do we turn this knowledge to our advantage?"

"This is all going wrong," Roper said.

"What do you mean?"

"Look," Roper said, "I find some connections between some robberies and decide to look into it. I decide that the same man—or person—planned them all. I also decide to try and find out who it is. Somehow, they find out about this and come after me. They also try for you, and they kill Gloria—and I don't even really know anything yet to make it worth all this effort."

"I thought you had a client?"

"I lied."

"Why?"

"I thought you might consider me a vigilante if I told you I was doing this on my own."

"Why are you doing it?"

"Well, among other reasons," Roper said, "if I'm right and I can catch the brain behind all these robberies it would be a feather in my cap."

"You're reputation is the best, Tal," Clint said, "and you're pretty successful."

"Not as successful as you might think," Roper said.

"What?"

"The Pinkertons are hard to compete with, and now there are a couple of similar organizations that have popped up. I'm just one man, Clint, and can't offer the kind of service they do."

"So you need something big, like this, to maybe put you into a position to compete."

"Right."

"So this was all a business decision?"

"Yes."

"I would have understood that."

"I'm sorry I lied," Roper said. "I've been in a real odd mood of late."

"Describe 'of late'?" Clint asked.

"The last few months," Roper said, "maybe even half a year."

Clint was surprised. Roper always presented a very controlled and confident front. To find that his friend's confidence might be shaken was . . . well, disconcerting.

"Why not move your operation?"

"To where?"

"New York comes to mind," Clint said. "You'd probably do real well there, attract a lot of new clients."

"You're probably right," Roper said. "A change of scenery is probably what I need, but now that I've started this—now that somebody had died because of it—I've got to finish it."

"Well, it seems to me we've got two options."

"What are they?"

"Go ahead with our plan to try and predict the next job."

"Or?"

"Or sit tight and wait until they make another attempt on one of us."

"And catch them at it?"

Clint nodded. "Hopefully, when they fail."

"That would mean leaving here and making ourselves visible again."

"Wrong."

"What?"

"That means me making myself visible again."

"Why you?"

"Because you're injured," Clint said. "You wouldn't be at your best, which would make you a stationary target. On top of that, if I'm the target you won't be able to cover me well enough."

Roper looked glum and said, "I can't argue with you there. So what do you suggest?"

"Well, first I need to get somebody here to watch my back," Clint said, "and then we can decide how best to proceed."

"Bat?"

"Maybe," Clint said.

"You could use Danny."

Clint looked dubiously at this suggestion.

"He's very young."

"He's trainable."

"I don't have time to train somebody," Clint said. "I need to know that I have somebody I can rely on covering my back."

"Well then, that part's going to be up to you."

"I'll give it some thought. Meanwhile, you probably need something to eat."

"I'm not hungry."

"Doesn't matter," Clint said. "You can't recover if you let yourself get run down." He stood up. "I'll go and get some food for both of us and bring it back. Maybe over dinner we can figure something out."

He walked to the door, then turned to look at Roper. He had no idea how close his friend had been to the dead woman, but he figured Roper needed a little bit of time by himself.

"Be back soon," Clint said.

He was out the door when he heard Roper shout, "Bring whiskey!"

This time, he wouldn't forget.

THIRTY

The girl whose real name was not "Ginger" read the telegram again. It didn't say what it really meant, but she was able to read between the lines. Joe Pittman was on his way to Denver. At least she wouldn't have to work with that idiot Halliday anymore. But this also meant that she had something to do before Pittman got here.

She tore up the telegram and burned it in her room—a cheap place she had been staying in since her arrival in Denver several weeks earlier. She then left and went to Bill Halliday's office. His office was in the same area as her rooming house, so she was able to walk there.

They had chosen Halliday for this project for two reasons. He wasn't successful at what he did, so he'd need the money. And he wasn't honest, so he'd have the contacts they needed.

When she walked into his office he stood up and shuffled his feet. She knew that her beauty intimidated him.

"Ginger," he said. It was the only name he knew her by.

"Mr. Halliday."

"Is there something else I can do for you?" he asked,

anxiously. He had never seen as much money as he had made these past few weeks working for her employer, Mr. Miller from Texas.

"Actually, no, Mr. Halliday," she said. "In fact, I'm here to tell you that we won't be requiring your services any further."

"Really?" he asked, disappointed. "Are you leaving?"

"No," she said, "you are."

"I'm not going—" He stopped short when she took the small derringer from her purse. "Hey, wait—" he said, his eyes bugging out, but it was too late. She pulled the trigger once, and then again. The small bullets struck him in two very vital areas, for she was very good with the weapon. He staggered, fell face forward onto his desk, then slid off and ended up on the floor, taking most of the contents of the desktop with him.

She put the gun away and walked around the desk. She examined everything on top of it, everything that had been dragged to the floor with him, and then went through the drawers. When that was done she searched the entire room. By the time she was finished she was satisfied that there was nothing in the office that would lead to her, or to her employer.

She looked down at him and, as a last thought, leaned over and went through his pockets. Sure enough he had most of the money he had been paid on him. She removed it and put it in her purse with the derringer.

His business was so unsuccessful that she knew it would be a long time before his body was discovered.

THIRTY-ONE

Clint and Roper ate in Roper's room, which—by virtue of being the best room in the Greek Hotel—was the larger of their two rooms. Clint had brought back two steak dinners from the café that had been highly recommended by Dimitri. He'd also brought back a pot of coffee, which they'd allowed him to remove from the restaurant when he mentioned Dimitri's name. Apparently, the Greek was very well respected in that community.

Lastly, Clint had brought back a bottle of whiskey, and they were drinking that with dinner.

"So tell me this?" Roper asked, after a few drinks.

"What?" He'd had a few drinks less than his friend.

"While you're walking around out there with a bull's-eye on you, your back covered by Bat Masterson or Wyatt Earp or Joe Whoever-You-Get, what am I supposed to be doing?"

"You're still supposed to be figuring out what their next job is going to be, just in case they don't come after me," Clint said. "Remember, Tal, you're still the brains of this outfit."

"Is that a fact?" Roper asked. "Seems to me you were the one smart enough not to get shot."

123

"You went up against at least two professional killers and you're still here to talk about it," Clint reminded him. "I think that's pretty good, don't you?"

"I got lucky."

"That may be," Clint said, "but being lucky is part of being good."

"You really believe that?"

"I do."

"You think you're alive after all these years because of luck?"

"Partially."

Roper took another drink and squinted across the room at Clint.

"Can I tell you why you're alive after all these years, my friend?"

"Sure," Clint said, "why not?"

"Because you have the best instincts of any man I've ever met," Roper said. "Hell, best of any man alive."

"Well, thanks, but—"

"I'm not finished!"

Clint fell silent.

"You are also the smartest man I know, the best man I've ever seen with a gun, and the best friend a man could ever have."

"That's really nice, Tal—"

"And all of that," Roper continued, gesturing with his glass so that he spilled some of the whiskey, "is why you're alive after all these years."

Clint remained silent, but apparently, this time, Roper had finished.

"Thanks."

"Shurrrre, ol' friend."

Clint removed the tray Roper's food had been on before he could upset it. When he went to grab the whiskey bottle Roper got it first.

"Ah-ah-ah," he said, "that's mine." The bottle was still half full, but what harm could Roper do to himself lying in his bed and finishing the rest off. If nothing else it would knock him out for the night.

"Fine," Clint said.

"If you get your glass," Roper said, "I'll share."

"No," Clint said, "I've had enough. I'm going to take the coffeepot to my room with me, if you don't mind?"

"Hell, no," Roper said. "I don't want no coffee, I just want the whiskey."

Clint couldn't remember the last time he'd seen his friend drunk. He certainly couldn't remember a time when his morale had been so low, or when he'd been so down on himself.

"Okay, Tal," he said, "you drink the whiskey, I'll drink the coffee, and we'll see who feels better in the morning."

"Ooh, a bet," Roper said. "Are we gonna have a bet on who feels better in the morning?"

"I don't think so."

"Why not?"

Clint was thinking, Because a fool and his money are soon parted, and that goes for a drunk, too.

"Okay," he said, instead, "I'll bet you a dollar I feel better than you do, come morning."

"It-sha bet!" Roper said.

"Good night, Tal."

" 'Night, buddy."

It was early to turn in, but Roper had drunk enough whiskey—and was probably going to consume more than enough—to put him right to sleep.

Clint wondered if he'd ever get his dollar, since his friend would surely never remember the bet.

THIRTY-TWO

Clint decided to send Bat Masterson a telegram first thing
in the morning and get him to Denver. Once Bat was there
he'd have somebody he trusted to watch his back. He'd
have to give Bat directions to the Greek Hotel, though.
Bat usually stayed at the Denver House, like Clint, when
he was there, but Clint didn't want anyone to see Masterson, or know he was there.

Clint also decided to move back to the Denver House.
If he was hiding out, how was anyone going to be able
to try for him, again? It was only Roper and Bat who
would have to stay at the Greek. And Bat would have to
forgo his usual dapper way of dressing so that people on
the streets wouldn't notice him, the way they always did.

Clint left his room that morning and walked to the end
of the hall to Roper's door. He noticed that the trays he'd
left outside the night before had been removed sometime
during the night. He knocked on Roper's door, then
knocked again when there was no answer. When there
was still no reply he was worried, so he opened the door
and entered.

The room smelled of whiskey and sweat, and Roper

was still passed out on his bed. The empty bottle had apparently rolled off the bed sometime during the night to the floor, and then rolled over against the wall. Roper was snoring softly, lying on his uninjured side. At least, in his condition, he was still able to avoid lying on his wounded shoulder.

Clint wondered if he should wake his friend, but decided to let him sleep it off for as long as it took. Later he could try to convince the man that he owed him a dollar for their bet, because he was damn sure Roper was going to wake up with a raging hangover.

He left the room, closing the door gently behind him, and went downstairs.

Naturally, the Greek was behind the desk and greeted him loudly.

"Ah, my friend. What are your plans for today?"

"I've got to go out for a while, Dimitri," Clint said.

"And how is our mutual friend?"

"He's still asleep. Well, actually, he's still passed out from drinking most of the bottle of whiskey last night. If I was you I'd just let him sleep, and then stay away from him for a while when he wakes up."

"Ah yes," Dimitri said, "after all that whiskey, the head, eh?" Dimitri slapped his own forehead to make his point.

"Yes," Clint said, "the head."

"Do not worry," Dimitri said. "I will be as quiet as a mouse."

"I'm sure Roper will appreciate it, Dimitri. Thanks."

"You will be back?"

"Yes," Clint said, "very soon."

Dimitri held his finger to his lips and then smiled broadly as Clint left.

• • •

Clint found the nearest telegraph office, rather than go
back to the one he had used while staying at the Denver
House. He sent off a concise message to Bat telling him
to come to Denver and wait at the train station. Clint
figured his friend would be there in two mornings. He just
hoped that nothing major happened between now and
then.

While there he sent another one to Rick Hartman, up-
dating him on what was happening and asking for any
information. He told the clerk where he was staying and
asked if he'd deliver any replies there.

"No," the man said, "not there. I don't go near that
area."

Clint frowned, wondering if the man was angling for
some money, then decided he wasn't. He was genuinely
afraid to go into the area where the Greek Hotel was lo-
cated.

"All right," Clint said, "just hold on to any replies and
I'll come and pick them up."

"That I can do," the man said. "Thanks for not—uh,
you know."

"Yeah," Clint said. "I know. If you don't go to that
area, you don't go. No problem."

There was not much left to do after that than wait for
Bat to arrive. He decided to go back to the Greek Hotel
and sit and brainstorm with Roper—that is, if the man's
brain was working, yet.

THIRTY-THREE

By the time Clint got back to the Greek Hotel Roper had awakened and had asked Dimitri to bring him a pot of coffee. This he found out from Dimitri as soon as he entered the building.

"How's he doing?" Clint asked.

"He said something about owing you a dollar," Dimitri said. "I did not understand."

"I do," Clint said. "Thanks, Dimitri."

He climbed the stairs, went to Roper's door, and knocked.

"Come ahead," Roper called.

Clint entered and saw Roper sitting on his bed. He had a cup of coffee on the end table next to him and was in the act of cleaning his gun.

"How's your head?"

"Yeah, yeah," Roper said, "I owe you a dollar."

"I'll collect later," Clint said. "Why are you cleaning your gun now?"

"It's something to do."

"You're not thinking about leaving here, are you?"

"No," Roper said, shaking his head. "I was shot in the

131

shoulder, not in the head. I know I'm of no use if I can't move around. Right now it's safer for both of us if I stay right here."

"Glad to hear it."

"Where do we stand?"

"Bat should be here in a couple of days," Clint said. "Until then I think I'll just lay low here, too."

"Maybe your gun can use some cleaning?"

"Maybe it can, at that," Clint said. "Any more coffee in that pot . . ."

The girl whose name was not really Ginger sat in the room of her cheap boardinghouse and looked around. She didn't have much choice but to lie low for a couple of days until Pittmam showed up. She couldn't accomplish much alone, especially since Clint Adams obviously didn't trust her. It was really too bad that she hadn't gotten to spend a few more nights with him. He sure knew how to treat a woman in bed. She was going to miss that touch of his. Pittman was nothing like Adams in bed. She frowned. Maybe she could train him, though. He was younger, and better looking, just a little bit selfish when it came to sex, like most men—except for Clint Adams.

She was going to feel real bad when it came time to kill him.

Joe Pittman packed his suitcase. It would be good to get away from El Paso, and from Miller himself, and see his woman again. It annoyed him when Miller referred to them as "the twins." Hell, they couldn't be more unlike twins if they tried. After all, they slept together. How many twins did that?

How would Henry Miller like it if Pittman kept calling him "Fat Gator?"

•   •   •

Bat Masterson picked up his mail from the hotel clerk in
Caldwell, Kansas, and read the telegram from Clint Adams right there and then. When he was done he folded it
and put it in his pocket.

"Prepare my bill," he told the clerk.

"Are you checking out?"

"I am."

"But . . . we thought you were staying longer."

"I was," Masterson said, "but it seems I'm not, anymore."

"Trouble?"

"Probably," Masterson said. "Get that bill ready and I'll
be back down in ten minutes."

"You're leaving that soon?"

"Some things just require quick action," he told the
man, and on the way up the stairs to his room he thought,
like responding to a call for help from a friend—especially when that friend was Clint Adams.

THIRTY-FOUR

After two days penned up inside the Greek Hotel it was a pleasure for Clint to get out and go to the railway station to meet Bat Masterson. Masterson had sent a telegram telling Clint when he'd arrive. Clint had asked Dimitri to have someone go to the telegraph office to pick up any replies, and Dimitri had done it himself. He'd been very impressed to learn that Clint actually knew Bat Masterson . . .

"You read the telegram?" Clint asked, when Dimitri gave it to him.

"Well," Dimitri said, "I had to make sure it was for you."

Clint looked at Roper, who only smiled.

"Will you introduce me when he gets here?" the Greek asked. "Will he be staying at my hotel?"

"I'm going to try to get him to stay here, Dimitri," Clint said. "We'll have to see if he goes along with it. And if he stays here then yes, I can introduce you."

Dimitri was very excited about that.

"I will give him my second best room," he said, "since my friend Roper already has the best one."

135

Clint didn't ask where his room showed up on the list . . .

Clint watched as the train pulled in, looking up and down the platform at the people who were also either waiting for someone to get off, or to get on, themselves. Actually, getting on and leaving Denver didn't sound like such a bad idea to him.

He felt certain that no one had followed him from the Greek Hotel. The only person he'd seen in the past two days besides Roper and the Greek was the young policeman, Danny Gibson. He was satisfied that no one knew that he and Roper were staying there.

When he saw Bat get off the train, carrying only one carpetbag, he went to intercept his friend, his hand held out in front of him.

Bat took the hand and said, "It's good to see you, Clint."

"Thanks for coming, Bat," Clint said. "I needed someone to watch my back and I couldn't think of anyone more qualified."

"I'm the only one who answered you telegram, huh?"

"That's true enough," Clint said, "but you were still my first choice."

"Okay," Bat said, "I'll accept that. Where are we headed, the Denver House?"

"No," Clint said, "I've got something else picked out for you, something kind of special."

"Why does that not fill me with anticipation?"

The girl whose name wasn't really Ginger saw Clint on the platform and melted into the background. Her hair was covered and she did not stand as proudly as she usually did, effectively hiding the lushness of her body beneath baggy clothes. She watched as Clint met a man she did not know coming off the train. Right behind that man came Joe Pittman, who stood and looked up and down the platform impatiently. She could not move, though, until Clint Adams had taken his colleague and left the platform, then she hurriedly moved toward Pittman.

"I have no time," he said, waving her away, mistaking her for a beggar.

"It's me, damn it!" she hissed.

He stared at her for several seconds and then said, "By God, it is you. What are you doing—"

"Never mind," she said. "Clint Adams was just here."

"What was he doing here?"

"Meeting someone who came off the train."

"Who?"

"A man," she said. "I didn't know him. He got off before you."

"*Just* before me?" Pittman asked.

"Yes," she said, "as a matter of fact, he was the man right in front of you."

"It seems you and Clint Adams have called for reinforcements."

"You know who that man was?"

"That was not just any man," Pittman said. "That was Bat Masterson."

"This is why I wasn't filled with anticipation," Bat said, when they were standing in front of the Greek Hotel.

"It's very clean inside," Clint said, "and the owner is a big fan of yours. He's dying to meet you, and he's been getting your room ready all day."

Bat gave Clint a baleful look.

"Come on," Clint said, "you'll see."

They entered the hotel together and stopped when Clint saw Dimitri bearing down on them.

"Is this him?" the Greek demanded. "Is this the famous Bat Masterson?"

"This is him, Dimitri," Clint said, slapping his friend on the back. "Bat Masterson, meet Dimitri Cosmocropoulas."

"Dimitri—" Bat said, not bothering with the last name.

"It is a pleasure, my friend, a great pleasure to meet you," Dimitri gushed, pumping Bat's hand enthusiastically. "I have prepared for you the best room in the house." Clint knew that was a lie. Dimitri probably meant the best unoccupied room in the house. "Please, I will take your bag and show you to your room. Come, come!"

He grabbed Bat's carpetbag and led the way to the stairs. Bat looked back at Clint once, who just shrugged, and then followed the Greek up the stairs to the second floor.

"Bring him to Roper's room when you're done, Dimitri!" Clint shouted.

THIRTY-FIVE

Bat, Clint, and Roper got together in Roper's room about half an hour later, when Bat was settled. Bat knocked and Clint let him in.

"You got away from him, huh?" Clint asked.

"I like him," Bat said. "He's a character. And you were right, the room is clean. It's not a bad place."

He walked over to Roper and put his hand out.

"How are you?"

"Getting there," Roper said. "Good to see you, Bat."

In truth Bat Masterson and Talbot Roper did not know each other all that well. In fact, except for the triumvirate of Bat Masterson, Wyatt Earp, and Luke Short, there were not many of Clint's friends who were close to each other.

"Understand you boys are having some trouble," Bat said. "How's that shoulder?"

"Hurts," Roper said, "but it's getting better."

"How'd they get you?"

"From behind."

"Bastards!" Bat said. He hated backshooters almost as much as Clint Adams did. "They'll get what's comin' to them."

"It's not even really them," Roper said, "but the man they work for."

"They'll all get it," Bat said. He turned to face Clint. "So what do you want me to do?"

"Just keep me from getting one in the back like Roper."

Bat spread his hands and said, "Consider it done."

She took Joe Pittman to her rooming house, where she had gotten him a room.

"You're kidding," he said.

"We have to keep a low profile."

"Not this low." He dropped his bag on the bed, causing it to squeak, and looked around the room.

"What's the word from Fat Gator?"

"He ever heard you call him that he'd kill you."

"No, he'd have me killed."

"He killed his own family," Pittman said.

"That's a rumor," she said. "Besides, even if he did, it was a long time ago. He hasn't killed anyone since. He had it done for him."

"He'd make an exception."

"All right, then," she said, "how's Mr. Miller?"

"Well, it's odd," he said, sitting on the bed. "He wasn't happy for a while, and then suddenly—when he found out Clint Adams was involved—his attitude totally changed."

"It's the challenge," she said.

"The what?"

"The challenge of outsmarting not only Roper, but Clint Adams, too," she said. "That's the way you men are. It's always the challenge. That's what gets so many of you killed, too."

"Is that a fact?"

"Yes."

He grabbed her and pulled her to him, but she resisted being thrown down on the bed.

"I'll show you a challenge."

She thought of being in bed with Clint Adams and then the thought of being in bed with Pittman did not excite her.

"Not now," she said, pulling her arm away. "We've got business to discuss."

"Hell with it, then," he said, in disgust. "You don't appeal to me, anyway, dressed like that."

"And you have travel smell on you," she said. "Take a bath and I'll meet you downstairs and take you for something to eat. We can talk then."

"Fine."

She turned and walked out of the room. He had an erection, but he'd never let her know it. Not until later, anyway.

"So my job is simple," Bat said. "Keep you alive while somebody tries to kill you."

"Simple to understand," Roper said, "but maybe hard to do."

"I've done it before," Bat said. "And tell me again why I have to stay here—not that I don't like it, now."

"We don't want the people involved *knowing* my back is being covered, let alone by who?" Clint said. "We want them to come after me so that you and I can take them."

"I get it," Bat said. "Then they lead to the leader." He looked at Roper, ". . . the man you're after."

"Right."

"Okay, I get it," Bat said.

"You don't have the big picture," Roper said.

Bat waved and said, "I don't need to know the big picture, as long as you fellas do. I'll just do my job, do what I'm told, and maybe I'll pick up the rest of it along the way."

"It'll come to you," Clint said. "It always does."

"That's the burden of having a brain that works," Bat said, "except the thing that's working right now is my stomach."

"Come on," Clint said. "I'll get you something to eat and we can discuss the logistics of keeping me alive."

THIRTY-SIX

Clint took Bat to the small café where he'd been getting the food to bring back to Roper.

"Ah, Dimitri's friend," the proprietor greeted them. "Will you eat with us tonight?"

"We'll take a table, yes," Clint said. "Thank you."

"Come this way," the man said. "Best table in the house for friends of my friend Dimitri."

Clint suspected that this man was Greek, as well, but he did not have as thick an accent as Dimitri.

"I will bring coffee," the man said.

"And steaks," Clint said, looking at Bat, who nodded. "Two steaks."

As the man hurried away Bat said, "Is Dimitri well known in this area?"

"He apparently has a lot of friends," Clint said.

"And is Dimitri's hand in a lot of pies?"

"It would seem so."

"Nice to know who I have as a big fan."

They made some small talk over coffee, each catching up on what the other was doing. It was not until Clint told Bat about Duke, though, that his friend displayed surprise and concern.

"You mean . . . you're not riding Duke, anymore?"

"Nope," Clint said. "Not for a few months, now."

"I always thought you'd be lost without that big black monster."

"I have been, sort of," Clint said, "but I've had to adjust."

"What have you replaced him with?"

"Nothing, yet," Clint said. "I'm just going from horse to horse."

"And where is he?"

"On a ranch just outside of Labyrinth," Clint said. "Rick Hartman arranged to have him looked after for me."

"Jesus," Bat said, "I can't imagine you without Duke."

"I couldn't, either," Clint said, "but I'm surviving."

"Did you ever think of putting yourself out to pasture with him?" Bat asked. "You know, you're starting to get up there yourself."

"Thank you very much for pointing that out to me," Clint said, "but I think I've got a ways to go before I get put out to pasture."

"Just something I thought about," Bat said, "with concern."

"Thanks for the concern," Clint said, "but I'll find another horse sooner or later."

"Not like that one, you won't."

Clint knew Bat was right, but he'd already come to terms with the loss of his big partner, and was trying to put it behind him. It wasn't like the big gelding had been killed, or died.

The steaks came and Bat expressed surprise at how good they were.

"You've been hobnobbing with the rich so long you forgot what it's like down here."

"Hey," Bat said, pointing his steak knife at Clint,

"you've forgotten who knows the Barbary Coast like the back of his hand."

"Oh yeah? When's the last time you were even on the Coast?"

"Last year," Bat said. "There was a big poker game down there."

"Did you ever leave the hotel?"

"Well," Bat said, "it was a marathon game, fifteen minute breaks only. There was no time to go out."

"Did you win?"

"Of course."

They talked some more about poker games, old friends, new friends, women, and finally came back around to the subject of what was going on presently in time to discuss it over coffee and pie.

"I didn't want to ask in front of Roper," Bat said, "but what's he gotten you into this time?"

Clint explained everything to Bat, who listened without interrupting until his friend was done.

"Why would he want to do this?" Bat asked. "I would have thought his reputation was secure."

"That's what I thought," Clint said. "I guess we were both wrong."

"No, maybe there's something wrong with him," Bat said. "A man can lose his confidence, you know."

"When did it happen to you?"

"It hasn't," Bat said, "yet."

They finished their pie and coffee, paid the bill, and started walking slowly back to the hotel.

"So, whoever Roper's mastermind is he's already tried to kill each of you once," Bat said.

"That's right."

"Doesn't make sense."

"Why not?"

"Seems to me a man like that would have an ego."

"So?"

"So his ego would want to outsmart the two of you," Bat said, "not have you killed by somebody else."

"Maybe this man has no ego."

"No," Bat said, "if he's planning these jobs and directing people to pull them, he has an ego. Believe me."

"Well then," Clint said, thoughtfully, "maybe that is what he's going to do now."

"Meaning?"

"Meaning he tried for us once," Clint said, "so maybe now he'll just try to outsmart us."

"And how do we find out if this is the case?"

"By doing just what I was going to do, anyway," Clint said.

"Walk around with a bull's-eye on your back?"

"Exactly."

"You know," Bat said, eyeing a couple who were kissing in a doorway, "one would think that was a condition you were damned tired of being in."

"Yeah," Clint said, "one would think that."

"Jesus," she said. "Quick, into this doorway."

"Wha—"

She pushed Joe Pittman into the doorway, pulled his head down so she could kiss him. She held the kiss a long time, and when she released him, Pittman was almost completely out of breath.

"What the hell—" he said. "First you don't want to sleep with me, and then you can't wait to kiss me—and suffocate me at the same time?"

She stuck her head out the door and said, "You didn't see them."

"Who?"

"Bat Masterson and Clint Adams were walking right toward us!"

"What?"

Now he leaned out the doorway and they both looked at the retreating backs of the two Western legends.

"What are they doing in this area?" he wondered aloud.

She laughed, then, and slapped his arm.

"The same thing we are," she said. "They're laying low where they think no one will find them."

Pittman looked her square in the eye.

"Are you thinking what I'm thinking?"

"Yes," she said, "but I'll do it. I'm more familiar with the area."

"And what about me?"

"You said you were hungry," she said, stepping from the doorway. "Go and get something to eat and I'll meet you back at the rooming house as soon as I find out where they're staying."

"But—" he started, but it was too late. She was running so that the two men would not get too far ahead of her.

Pittman looked around, feeling lost for a moment. She'd told him where to find the café and he knew where the hotel was. He finally decided he could go on to the café, eat, and still find his way back the hotel.

As he walked he realized this might have been the break they were needing, running into the two men without having to look for them. All they needed now was word back from Henry Miller on what he wanted them to do—and that reminded him that he needed to send his boss a telegram.

Now where was the damned telegraph office?

THIRTY-SEVEN

The girl followed Clint and Bat back to the Greek Hotel. It was funny, but when she first arrived in Denver and found that area, she thought about staying there until she found her rooming house, which was only blocks away. How ironic to find that she'd been staying that close to where Clint Adams had come when he left the Denver House Hotel.

Once she saw them go in the front door of the hotel she toyed briefly with the idea of going inside, but decided that would have been too risky. Instead, she turned and left, going back the way she had come to find Joe Pittman.

Clint and Bat entered the hotel, unaware that they had been followed back. It would be a lesson for both of them when they found out about it later on. They'd realize that if she'd had a gun with her they both could have been dead, shot in the back by a woman. Bat would particularly feel bad, since his job, after all, *was* to watch Clint Adams's back.

They entered the hotel still deep in conversation.

• • •

"So when do we start?" Bat asked.

"Today," Clint said. "I'm going to go back to the Denver House and check back in. Then I'll have something to eat in the dining room. Then maybe I'll read a paper in the lobby. By that time everyone should know that I'm back."

"And what do I do in the meantime?"

"You do something you've never tried to do before."

"And what's that?"

"Go unnoticed."

"With these looks?" Bat asked. "I'll try."

"Oh, and there's one more thing you should be aware of."

"What's that?'

"A detective named Donovan."

"What's his claim to fame?"

"He's investigating both the attempts on me and Roper," Clint said, "only he may not be so anxious to find the guilty parties."

"Is he dirty?"

"That's the word we got."

"From a reliable source?"

"From another police officer," Clint said, "a young man who sort of idolized Roper."

"Ah . . ."

At that moment Dimitri appeared from somewhere in back of the front desk, saw Bat and started to gush again. It took a few moments for them to finally get away from him and go upstairs.

As they walked down the hall toward Roper's room Clint said, "You know all about being idolized, don't you?"

"Why Clint," Bat said, "I knew we were friends, but . . ."

•   •   •

She found Pittman at the café. He was actually relieved when he saw her walk in, because he was no longer sure he would be able to find his way back to the rooming house.

"That was quick," he said.

"It's amazing," she said, sitting across from him. She reached out and snagged a potato from his plate. "They're actually staying at a hotel just a few blocks from where we are."

"That's quite a coincidence."

"Well, you know what Fat Gator says about coincidence."

"Right," Pittman said. " 'Never take it for granted.' "

"No, he says 'never look it in the mouth,' or something like that."

"Never mind. What we have to do next is send him a telegram and see what *he* wants us to do next."

"Right."

"If we need some help do we still have that detective working for us?" Pittman asked.

"Um . . . well, we did, but we don't anymore—"

"Celeste," he said, using her real name for the first time, "did you kill him, already with that little gun of yours?"

"I'm afraid I did," she said, with a smile.

He sat back in his chair and stared at her.

"Who else did you kill?"

"No one," she said, looking indignant, but then she added, "Just a prostitute nobody will miss."

"A prostitute?" he asked. "Why did you have to kill her?"

"So I could take her place and get close to Clint Adams."

Now he sat forward.

"How close did you get to him?"

She reached out and stroked his hand.

"Jealous?"

He eased his hand away and said, "Worried. This means Adams can recognize you."

She smiled, reached for his hand again, and said, "Not necessarily."

THIRTY-EIGHT

When Celeste took Joe Pittman to the telegraph office she had been using to stay in contact with Miller, there was already a telegram there waiting for them. They took it, paid for it, and waited until they were outside to read it.

"He wants us to do nothing until a messenger reaches us," Pittman said, with a puzzled frown.

"Is that all it says?"

He handed it to her and she read it. It was one line: DO NOTHING UNTIL MESSENGER ARRIVES.

"Obviously he's sending someone, probably by train, with a message . . . but why?" Pittman asked. "Why didn't he just tell me so I could tell you?"

"I don't understand, either," she said. "What do we do now? We know where Adams is, and Roper is probably there, too."

"He doesn't want either of them killed."

"What?"

"That's what he told me before I left."

"Why didn't you tell me that before?"

He looked at her and said, "It didn't come up."

She glared at him.

153

"We'll have to send a reply," he said, turning to go back inside.

"Wait," she said, grabbing his arm.

"Why?"

"Let's think about this."

"What's to think about?"

"What if we didn't pick up this telegram yet?"

"But we did."

"Yes, but what if we *didn't*?"

"What are you getting at?"

"Let's go back to the rooming house and I'll tell you."

"But we can send a reply while we're here."

"Just listen to what I have to say, Joe," she said. "Hear me out, then if you still want to send a reply, I'll come back here with you."

"That'll be good," he said, half under his breath, "because I don't think I could find it again by myself."

Clint and Bat dropped in on Roper one more time before heading for the Denver House Hotel. Bat had stopped in his room and had changed into the worst clothes he had. Unfortunately, they were still cleaner than anything anyone else on the street would be wearing. However, he wasn't in a dark suit with a boiled white shirt, and he wasn't wearing a derby.

"What are you supposed to be?" Roper asked him.

"In disguise."

"Well," Roper said, "it doesn't work. You still look like you."

"To you, maybe," Clint said, "but it's good enough for our purposes."

"So now's the time you go out with a target painted on your back?" Roper asked Clint.

"Now's the time."

Roper looked at Bat.

"Keep him alive for a while, will you?"

"As long as I can," Bat said.

"I wish I was going out there with you."

"You'll be out there soon enough," Clint said. "Just relax, don't aggravate your wound, and it might be sooner than you think."

"Yeah, right."

Clint and Bat headed for the door.

"Check for telegrams, will you?" Roper asked. "I'm still waiting for one or two replies."

"Will do," Clint said. "I'll see you soon."

On the street they agreed to share a cab to within walking distance of the Denver House. From that point on Bat would become Clint's shadow.

"Just remember," Clint said, "I've been followed before, so keep an eye out."

"Right, Chief."

"And it might even be a woman."

"Oh, even better," Bat said. "A pretty one?"

"Beautiful."

"I'll definitely keep an eye out."

They had the driver pull up three blocks from the hotel and got out.

"From here on we don't meet or talk unless it's back at the Greek House," Clint said.

"Or in case of an emergency," Bat said.

"Like what?"

"Like if someone is aiming a gun at your back and I have to yell 'Look out!' Like that."

"Do me a favor?"

"Sure, whatever you like."

"If that happens," Clint said, "shoot first and shout later?"

Bat smiled and said, "That's a promise."

THIRTY-NINE

"Back with us, Mr. Adams?" the desk clerk asked. It was the same one who had checked him in and out. Clint wondered if anyone else but him worked the front desk, anymore.

"I missed the food," he said, "and the clean sheets."

"Same room all right?" the man asked.

"If you don't mind," Clint said, "somebody tried to shoot me the last time I was in that room."

"Oh, yes," the clerk said, flushing with embarrassment, "of course. How stupid of me. I'll give you a room on another floor, entirely . . ." He turned and grabbed a key. "And in another section."

"Thanks," Clint said. "I appreciate that."

"I'll inform the manager that you are back in the house," the clerk said. "He will, in turn, tell security."

"I appreciate that," Clint said, without mentioning that he had brought along his own security, this time. He took the key. "I'll find my own way."

"Of course," the clerk said, "and welcome back. Oh, by the way."

"Yes?"

"A couple of telegrams came for you after you left," the clerk said. "We didn't know where to forward them, so we simply held them. I'll get them for you."

Clint waited, then accepted the telegrams, and went up to his room. He didn't read them until he was inside. One was from Wyatt Earp. He was somewhere in Alaska, and Clint's original telegram had been forwarded to him. It said that if Clint really needed him he'd hop the next steamer, but that it would take him a while to get there. Clint decided to get back to Wyatt as soon as he could and tell him to stay put.

The other telegram was for Roper, but Clint read it, anyway. It was very interesting, and he was going to have to get it to Roper as soon as possible. He might even have to go back to the Greek Hotel sooner than he thought.

Before he could make a decision, though, there was a knock on the door. He expected either the manager or the security man, but he answered it with gun in hand, hand behind his back, anyway.

It was neither of them.

It was Detective Donovan.

"You're a very good detective," Clint said. "I just checked back into the hotel a few minutes ago"

"I know," Donovan said. "I left word that I was to be notified if you did, just in case."

Word would have had to travel pretty fast to get to Donovan that quickly.

"Can I come in," he asked, "or are you gonna shoot me in the hall."

Clint brought the gun around from behind his back and pointed it at the floor.

"Come on in, Detective."

He backed away and let the man enter. He didn't have a two-room suite, this time, just a single room. Still, it was larger than most rooms he had ever had, and he was able to put some room between himself and the detective. In examining the man critically he could see that he had a gun in a shoulder holster beneath his left arm. He hadn't removed his holster, yet, so instead of putting his gun he simply holstered it. He could see by the look in Donovan's eyes that the significance of that had not escaped him.

"What can I do for you, Detective?"

"This is just a courtesy call," Donovan said. "I thought maybe you'd left our fair city."

"Not yet."

"And Roper?" Donovan asked. "Is he still around?"

"Around and healing nicely."

"Good, good," Donovan said, "that's good to hear. No more attempts on your lives?"

"Not a one."

"Also good," Donovan said.

"If you don't have any other questions," Clint said, "I'd like to get settled."

"I might have one or two," Donovan said. "Give me a minute."

Clint gave the man the minute he asked for, but did not take his eyes off of him. If Donovan was there to kill him he was going to have to be *very* good with that gun under his arm. The man's jacket was buttoned, however, so Clint wasn't really expecting any kind of an attempt.

"I was wondering," Donovan said, finally, "why you'd come back to a hotel where somebody had tried to kill you?"

"It's still the best hotel in town," Clint said, then added, "that I can afford, that is."

"I see. You wouldn't, by any chance, be dangling yourself as bait to try and catch the fellas who tried to gun you and your friend?"

"Now why would I do that, Detective?" Clint asked.

"Catching those desperados is your job, not mine."

"I'm glad you realize that."

"And since you're around here so much," Clint added, "I think I feel safer here than I would any other hotel in town."

Donovan smiled.

"I'll take that as a compliment."

"That's how it was meant."

The two men stared at each other across the length of the room for a few moments before Donovan turned slightly toward the door.

"I guess I'll be going, then."

"By the way, have you made any progress finding who killed that young prostitute?"

"How did you know about the dead whore?"

"That kind of news travels," Clint said. "I heard you were looking into that, too. I guess they give you all the hard ones, huh?"

"Usually," Donovan said, "they give me the dead ones."

"Really?" Clint said. "I guess that means Roper and I were the exceptions, huh?"

Donovan smiled, opened the door, and said, "So far."

He left.

FORTY

Joe Pittman came out of the Greek Hotel and walked across the street to where Celeste was waiting for him.

"He's gone."

"What?"

"Checked out."

"How do you know?"

"I looked at the register," Pittman said. "Nobody was there, so I looked. He was checked in, and he checked out."

"What about Roper?"

"Not checked in."

"He's in there, though," she said. "I know it. And Masterson?"

"Checked in, and still there."

"So what happened to Adams? Is he still in there, too? And if so why bother to check out formally? To throw us off?"

"He doesn't know about us."

"He knows about somebody," she said. "We all sort of know about each other, Joe."

"Look," Pittman said, "we're out of our element, here.

161

I don't know how I let you talk me into this. We should have notified Miller right away about what was going on."

"Look," Celeste said, "this is our chance to get out from under him, don't you see? If we kill Roper *and* the Gunsmith our reputations will be made. We won't need Fat Gator anymore."

"You're the one who wants a reputation as a killer," Pittman said. "I just want money."

"We can both get what we want, Joe."

"How? We don't know this town and you killed the only local who was helping us."

"No," she said, "I didn't."

"What are you talking about?"

"There's somebody else?"

"Who?"

"Come on," she said, stepping from her doorway, "I'll introduce you."

After Donovan left Clint he had a premonition that he was going to end up killing the detective—that he'd *have* to kill the man before this was all over. It was in the way Donovan had stood and looked across the room at him. He'd had the feeling then that if the man's jacket *hadn't* been buttoned, he might have gone for his gun then and there. So it didn't happen then, but it would probably happen later.

He looked around the room. If, as Roper put it, he had painted a target on his back, it wasn't going to do any good to stay in the room. He had to get out on the streets and let people see it. He had to get out there where they could take their shot, and Bat could do his job and save his life.

He put on his hat, lifted his gun, and dropped it in his holster, making sure it was nice and loose, and then left the room.

FORTY-ONE

He couldn't see Bat Masterson as he exited the hotel, which was good. If he couldn't see him, maybe no one else would, either.

Clint felt he had to do more than simply walk around. That might make it too obvious that he was dangling himself as bait. Instead, he went back to both of the telegraph offices he had used to see if there were any telegrams being held for him. He had also checked with the front desk of the Denver House, but they didn't have any more messages for him.

Neither did either of the offices, but that was okay. The point was to be *going* somewhere. After the two telegraph offices he decided to get some lunch. He found a small café and went inside. He got a table against the back wall and kept an eye on the door while he ate. Hopefully, Bat was doing the same thing from the outside.

Several people came in and were seated, two couples and one man alone, but none of them seemed to be paying any special attention to him.

Clint had two faces he felt he could be on the lookout for. One was Detective Donovan's, and the other was the woman who had called herself Ginger. There had to be others, however, that he wouldn't recognize. Surely, the shooters who had almost killed Roper, if they were still in Denver. As professionals they might have left town immediately after the shooting, but also as professionals they might have wanted to stay around to finish the job— or maybe take a new job.

As he left the café he looked around carefully, as a man with his reputation would most likely do, in any case. He could not spot Bat, or anyone else, following or observing him. For all he knew he could have been alone there. There were other people walking up and down the street, of course, but none who gave any indication that they were the least bit interested in him.

For want of somewhere else to go he started back to his hotel, but part of the way there he was suddenly struck with an idea. Instead of waiting, maybe he could do more good by pushing.

He altered his course and went, instead, to the police station where both Danny Gibson and Detective Donovan worked.

"Clint."

He turned at the sound of his name as he entered the station and saw Danny standing off to one side. The young man was in uniform.

"Danny," he said, walking over to him. "I thought you'd be out on the street."

"I'm on my way," Danny said. "Is there something wrong? Something I could do for you or Mr. Roper?"

"No, no," Clint said, "nothing's wrong. I just thought that since Detective Donovan has paid me so many visits I'd return the favor and pay him one. Is he in, by any chance?"

"I think so. I could get him—"

"No," Clint said, "you go on out to work. I'll stop by the desk and let them tell him I'm here."

"Are you sure?"

"I'm positive," Clint said. "Go ahead. I don't want him to see us together, anyway."

"All right," Danny said. "I was going to stop by the hotel to see Mr. Roper later, anyway."

"That's a good idea, Danny," Clint said. "See you then."

Danny nodded and left the station. Clint walked up to the front desk, which was manned by a uniformed officer wearing sergeant's stripes.

"Can I help ya?" the man asked.

"I'm here to see Detective Donovan."

"Got an appointment?"

"No," Clint said, "but I think he'll see me."

"Zat so?" The sergeant eyed him curiously, maybe wondering if he was a drinking buddy of the detective's.

"Wait here," he said, finally. "I'll let 'im know you're here."

"Thank you."

"What's your name?"

"Adams," he said, "Clint Adams."

If it meant anything to the sergeant he didn't let on. He left the desk and disappeared down a hall. When he reappeared Donovan was walking right behind him.

"Mr. Adams!" he said, expansively. "What a nice surprise. Did you come all the way over here just to see me? Or are you visiting your young friend, Officer Gibson?"

Clint stared at him for a minute.

"Don't look so surprised, Mr. Adams," Donovan said. "After all, I am a detective."

Donovan turned to the sergeant and said, "It's okay, Sarge. This man is a friend of mine."

"Sure," the sergeant said, looking bored.

"Doesn't his name ring a bell with you?" Donovan asked. "Clint Adams? The Gunsmith? A legend of the West?"

The sergeant continued to look bored.

"Sergeant McNulty doesn't impress easy," Donovan said to Clint. "Come on back with me and we'll have a talk. That is why you're here, isn't it? To talk?"

"That's exactly why I'm here."

"I thought so. Come on."

Donovan led Clint down the hall to an office that smelled stale and boozy. Clint marvelled at the fact that Donovan did not seem to be trying to hide his drinking. He was even weaving a bit as Clint followed him to his office.

"Have a seat," Donovan invited. "I'll just close this door so we can have some privacy."

Donovan had to pass behind Clint to close the door and Clint craned his neck to keep the man in sight. Donovan seemed to find this amusing and chuckled as he closed the door.

FORTY-TWO

"What brings you here?" Donovan asked from behind his desk. He wasn't wearing his jacket and his shoulder harness was very much in evidence. The gun in the holster looked like a .32 caliber pistol to Clint. Smallish caliber, but still deadly in the right hands.

"Games."

"What about them?"

"I don't like playing them."

"Who's been playing games?"

"You, me, whoever it is you're working for."

"The city of Denver?"

"Not who I had in mind."

"That's who I work for."

"See what I mean? We're playing games." Clint leaned forward. "You work for a lot of people, Detective, probably mostly for yourself. Maybe you're just trying to make a little money on the side."

"A little extra money is good," Donovan said.

"Yes, but I don't think you care how you get it," Clint said. "For instance, covering up for a couple of shooters. Maybe even doing a little bit of work for the same people who hired them."

Donovan eyed Clint for a few moments, then sat back in his chair.

"You know," he said, "you're a big man on the trail and in cow towns, but this is a city, Adams. You're out of your element here." He sat forward. "This is where I excel."

"At what? Drinking?"

Donovan smiled.

"You're trying to get my goat," he said. "Yeah, drinking is one of the things I'm good at."

"What are the others?"

"Making people disappear."

"Like prostitutes?"

"You think I killed that whore, Gloria?"

"If you didn't," Clint said, "you know who did, and you're covering for them. You're also covering for the people who want me and Roper dead."

Donovan sat back again.

"Maybe you're in the clear, there."

"How's that?"

"Maybe whoever wanted you dead doesn't want you dead, anymore."

"And why would that be?"

"How would I know?" Donovan said. "I'm just . . . supposing. Suppose they didn't want you dead, anymore. What do you think the reason would be?"

"I'd think," Clint said, slowly, "that somebody with a large ego would rather outsmart us than kill us."

Donovan didn't react.

"Nothing can happen here," he said, finally. "This is a police station. But out there . . ." He pointed out his window. "Out there a lot could happen, Adams. I'd advise you to be real careful."

Clint stood up and Donovan stiffened in his chair, eyeing him warily.

"I came here to tell you that I'm on to you," Clint said. "That's all."

"That's enough, don't you think?" Donovan asked. "Enough to change the whole complexion of the game."

"There's no game, Donovan," Clint said. "Not anymore. Now it's for real."

"I couldn't agree more," the detective said. "And now I think it's time you left my office."

"With pleasure."

Clint opened the door and Donovan said, "By the way."

Clint turned and looked at him.

"It's just as dangerous out there for policemen as it is for civilians like you," Donovan said. "Especially young policemen."

"What are you saying?"

"I'm saying good-bye, Mr. Adams."

"If you do anything to Danny Gibson, Donovan," Clint said, "if you hurt him—"

"You can't threaten me in my own office, Adams," Donovan said. "I could lock you up for that."

The two men matched stares.

"Besides," Donovan said, coming around his desk and ushering Clint out the door, "I don't know what you're talking about. You might as well be talking Greek."

He closed the door in Clint's face, leaving him standing out in the hall.

Clint went back to his hotel, still unable to spot Bat Masterson, who was being much better at his job than even Clint had thought he would.

At the hotel he went into the bar to have a beer and consider the things that had been said in Donovan's office. More word games on the part of the detective, but he obviously knew that Danny Gibson had been helping Clint and Roper, and he obviously was working for the

people who tried to kill Roper. And he obviously had no
fear of Clint Adams, at all. He was, after all, in his own
element.

Clint was halfway through his beer, replaying the conversation in his head, when he realized how stupid he was.
The last words Donovan had said to him as he all but
pushed him out the door. "You might as well be talking
Greek."

Clint stood up and rushed out of the bar, across the
lobby and out the door. Of course, he hadn't seen anyone
who was a danger to him all day, and nobody had made
an attempt on him because it wasn't him they were after.
Not yet, anyway. Not while Roper was injured and an
easier target at the Greek Hotel.

FORTY-THREE

When Clint came running out of the Denver House Hotel
Bat Masterson knew something was amiss. He fell into
place as they raced for a cab and gave the driver the address of the Greek Hotel. On the way Clint told Bat about
his conversation with Donovan and how the man had
made it very clear that he knew where Roper was.

"How could he?" Bat asked.

"I don't know," Clint said, "but if he knows, others
know, too. If we get there too late . . ."

When they rushed into the Greek House the first thing
they saw was Danny Gibson lying on the lobby floor.

"Dan!" Clint swore.

The young policeman was dead, shot in the chest twice
by what appeared to be a small caliber weapon.

"Better check behind the desk," Clint said to Bat. He
had his gun out and Bat followed his lead. He went
around behind the desk and stopped short.

"Same here," he said, looking down at Dimitri. He'd
been shot also, but with a larger caliber gun.

"Upstairs," Clint said, and then both ran up the stairs.

As they ran down the hall they could see that the door
to Roper's room was wide open. They entered and saw
the blood on the bed, but there was no body.

"What happened here?" Clint demanded out loud.

Clint looked out the window. It was a sheer drop. Roper
could not have gotten out that way.

"Looks like maybe they grabbed him," Bat said.
"Maybe they're gonna use him to get to you."

"Bat," Clint said, "if they knew about this place they
probably know about you, too."

"You're probably right."

"If Roper's alive," Clint said, "they have things all their
own way."

"And if he's dead?"

Clint looked at his friend and said, "Then they'll be
sorry."

They didn't wait at the hotel for the police because they
were afraid they'd be taken into custody. If that happened
they might end up at the mercy of Detective Donovan,
unarmed and in a cell. Or Roper would end up dead because they couldn't get to him.

They went back to the Denver House Hotel, figuring
they'd be contacted there. Sooner or later someone would
walk into the Greek Hotel and discover the bodies of
Danny Gibson and Dimitri Cosmocropoulas. Clint was
sorry to leave the two men lying there like that, but felt
that he didn't have much of a choice in the matter.

They discussed going to the police station where Donovan worked, but thought there was little chance he'd be
there. And then there was still the very real possibility of
ending up in a cell without their guns.

"Any messages?" Clint asked the desk clerk.

"One," the man said, finally a different clerk from the
one Clint was used to seeing.

Clint accepted it without a word and he and Bat walked off to the side to read it right there in the lobby. It wasn't a telegram, but a handwritten note.

"What's it say?" Bat asked.

" 'Roper is in a cabin by the lake,' " Clint read. " 'Better get there quick before it's too late.' " He looked at Bat. "There are directions."

"It's a trap."

"Of course it is."

"But we're going anyway, aren't we?"

"Of course we are."

Bat made a face. "I knew you'd say that."

FORTY-FOUR

It was called Cherry Creek Lake. Clint had never heard of it, but the directions were very precise. They rented a buckboard, figuring they'd probably need it to transport Roper back to the city—dead or alive.

When they came to the lake they had to abandon the buckboard and take to a footpath. By then it was starting to get dark.

"You know if I get killed doing this I'll never forgive you," Bat said, as they moved along the path.

"I'm sorry, Bat."

"Forget it," Bat said. "There are worse ways to get killed than while watching your back."

"Thanks."

They kept moving along the path, keeping alert even though Clint figured nothing was going to happen until they actually reached the cabin. It was too good a setup to ruin, getting them into a cabin out by a lake where it was deserted and quiet.

"How many you figure?" Bat asked.

"At least five."

"We've had worse odds."

"One will be a woman."

"Don't know if that makes it better or worse," Bat said.

Up ahead they suddenly saw a light as it got even darker. When they got closer they saw that the light was coming from the window of a cabin.

"Wonder what this place is?" Bat asked.

"Maybe somebody's vacation spot," Clint said. "Donovan's, maybe."

"He'd use his own place?"

"Why not? It's pretty deserted."

"And quiet."

"Too quiet."

When they reached the cabin they hesitated.

"This is iffy," Bat said. "Either Roper's in there, or a bunch of men with guns."

"That sounds iffy, all right."

"Want me to go in first?' Bat asked.

"No," Clint said. "My responsibility."

"I know," Bat said. "I just thought it polite to ask."

"Appreciate it."

They approached the front door, half expecting a hail of bullets from every direction. When nothing came Clint reached for the door and opened it. They stepped inside. In the light from a storm lamp they saw somebody lying on a cot against the wall, with his back to them.

"Check him," Clint said. "I'll watch the door." He drew his gun.

Bat moved to the man on the cot.

"It's Roper, and he's alive."

"Okay, then," Clint said. "We're all here. Now what?"

The answer came from outside.

"Adams!" a voice called. It sounded like Detective Donovan.

"That you, Donovan?"

"It's me," Donovan called back. "I see you found your way here."

"We're here," Clint said. "Now what?"

"Throw out your guns."

"You're crazy," Clint called back. "We throw out our guns we're as good as dead."

"You're as good as dead, anyway," Donovan said. "Why not make it easy on yourself?"

"Who else is out there with you?" Clint asked.

There was some hesitation, then Donovan said, "Enough guns to handle you and your friend, Masterson."

"I'm guessing five, Donovan," Clint said. "You, the people you work for, the men who shot Roper. Four, five at the outside. Am I right?"

His question was greeted by silence.

Joe Pittman said, "How does he know we're five?"

"He doesn't know," Celeste said. "He's guessing."

"Well," Pittman said, "it's too good a guess."

"Don't worry," Donovan said. "We can handle them." He looked at the two men standing alongside him.

"You two should have had Roper outside his office," Celeste said.

"He's got good instincts," one of them said. "That's all that saved him."

"It won't save him again," the other said.

"Then go in and finish them," Celeste said. The telegram from Miller telling them *not* to kill Roper and Clint was burning a hole in her pocket. "And don't mess it up, this time."

Donovan said, "Don't worry."

She could smell the whiskey on him, but he seemed able to function.

"I'll worry until we can send a telegram to our employer saying that they're dead."

Donovan smiled. "That time is only minutes away." He turned to the two men. "Let's go."

As they started for the cabin Pittman said to Celeste, "What if we've underestimated Adams and Masterson."

"No chance of that," she said. "If we have a problem it will be because we overestimated Donovan."

Pittman drew his own gun and Celeste did the same. They were their own aces in the hole.

FORTY-FIVE

"So?" Bat asked Clint. "Are we going out or are they coming in?"

"Going out is a bad idea, don't you think?" Clint asked. "Besides, if we do that we leave Roper in here, and he's vulnerable."

"Right," Bat said, "so we all stay together, right here. Let them come in and get us."

"Right."

Both checked their guns then looked around the cabin. It was one room with several windows, but only one door. One of the windows—the one in the back wall—had wooden shutters that opened in. Clint walked to it and closed the shutters. Now they only had to deal with two windows in the front wall, one on either side of the door.

"We need to move Roper so he can't be seen from the windows," Clint said.

"Move him? Or the whole cot?"

"Is he unconscious?"

"Yes."

"Let's move the whole cot."

They hurriedly dragged the cot across the floor and

found a dead space where he couldn't be seen from one of the windows.

"Now what?" Clint asked aloud.

"I guess we each take a window and wait."

They each went to a window and looked out, guns in hand. It was dark and they couldn't see anything.

"Better douse the lamp," Bat said. "We'll be able to see out better, and they won't see so well inside."

"Good idea.

Clint blew out the lamp and returned to his window.

"What if they burn us out?" Bat asked.

"Then we'll have to go out with guns blazing and just see what happens," Clint said. "Actually, that seems most likely, don't you think? It's what I'd do."

"Me, too."

"Guess we better be ready for it."

They both turned and looked at Roper. They both knew that if they didn't get him out of there and to a hospital he might die. Dragging him from the Greek Hotel had aggravated his wound, but at least it had stopped bleeding—for now.

"We can't just wait," Clint finally said. "We've got to act."

"Okay," Bat said. "One inside and one outside. Who's going out?"

"Me," Clint said. "You stay and watch out for Roper."

"Okay. I'll cover you from the window."

Clint peered out his window. The moon was not full, but it was giving off some light. It would not be pitch dark out there, not once his eyes adjusted to having the lamp extinguished inside. When he was able to make out shapes and sizes outside he moved toward the door. With no light inside, he might just be able to open it and slip out without being seen.

"Ready?" he asked Bat.

"I'm ready if you are."

Clint opened the door.

Donovan and the other two men were moving closer to he house. Suddenly, the light inside went out.

"Wait," Donovan said.

"What for?" one of the other men asked. "They're rapped in there, whether they have light or not."

"Let's just give them some time—"

"Look," one of the men said, "you're the law, Donovan. This is our business. Why don't you just stay here if ou're afraid?"

Donovan looked at the two men he knew as Willis and Barlow. It was Barlow who had spoken.

"Okay, then," Donovan said. "Why don't the two of ou go ahead?"

Barlow looked at Willis and said, "Come on."

As the two men started for the house Donovan decided o circle around and come at it from behind. It was his abin, so he knew there was a window back there.

Barlow and Willis were moving right for the front of he house. They were taking the direct route, apparently, ght through the front door. Donovan figured he knew nough about Clint Adams to know that they were in for big surprise.

arther from the house Joe Pittman said, "I'm getting loser."

"Joe, why don't we let Donovan and the other two handle it?" she said. "We can still take credit for the kill."

"If we're going to do that," Pittman said, "we'll have get rid of those other two once they've done the job." He'd learned that much from "Fat Gator" Miller. Clean p your mess.

"You have a point," she said. "All right, I'm coming,

too." She took out her little gun, the one she'd used to kill Danny Gibson. He was shocked to be shot by a woman. She saw it in his face, just before the life drained out of him. Pittman was holding the gun he'd used to shoot the Greek, Dimitri.

"What about Donovan?" he asked. "Do we let him walk away from this?"

"My thought is no," she said. "The whole mess won't be cleaned up unless we get rid of him, too."

"Agreed," Pittman said. "All right, then. Let's get closer."

It all happened very quickly. As Clint opened the front door and stepped outside, he came face-to-face with two men holding guns. The three of them stopped just short of bumping into each other. The last thing the two men had expected was for the trapped men to try to get out of the cabin.

"Jesus—" Barlow said, scared shitless by the appearance of Clint.

"Holy—" Willis said, and started to bring up his gun.

Clint was the quickest. He shot Barlow while the man was still trying to voice his surprise. There was the sound of breaking glass as Bat thrust his gun right through it and shot Willis before he could recover. Willis pulled the trigger of his gun as he was going down. The muzzle flash of that gun and his own blinded Clint for a moment.

Behind him, Bat heard the sound of more glass breaking as Donovan knocked the glass from the back window. He saw a shape framed by the front window and took a shot, but Bat was moving already. He threw himself forward, diving to the floor, rolled, came up on one knee and fired. The bullet went through the broken window and struck Donovan in the forehead. It knocked him back, tore off most of the top of his head, and left him lying in the dirt on his back.

"Bat!" Clint shouted, still seeing the remnants of the dual muzzle flashes before his eyes.

Bat came out the door and stopped behind Clint.

"I got another one, tried to come up behind us."

"Stay with Roper," Clint said. "Make sure these fellas are dead."

"Where are you—" Bat started, but Clint was already running, and Bat realized he wanted to be able to catch any others who were still out there.

At the sound of the shots both of the twins stopped. They saw the scene in front of the house as it was illuminated by muzzle flashes. They watched as both of their men went down, and then there was a shot from inside the house. In the interest of self-preservation, they ran . . .

Clint couldn't see them but he could hear them ahead of him, running along the path. His momentary blindness from the muzzle flashes was gone. The path was a winding one, but when it straightened, he could see them ahead of him, running. A man and a woman. The woman he had known as Ginger, and a man he probably had never known.

"Stop!"

The woman turned to look back, tripped on an upturned root, and went sprawling. Her fall caused her to clip the heels of the man running ahead of her, and he, too, fell. In moments, Clint was on them.

"No, wait," the man said, his tone panicky.

He rolled over, holding his hands out in front of him, a gun in one hand. Clint could not be sure what his intention was, and he took no chances. He fired. The man clutched his midsection and dropped his gun.

"No!" Celeste/Ginger cried out. "You killed him!"

"Take it easy—"

She turned on him, still on the ground, and brought her gun around. Her intention was clear, and he shot her, as well. He hated like hell to shoot a woman, but it was much better than being shot by one.

She died instantly. The man writhed on the ground and Clint went to him.

"Who sent you?" Clint asked. "Who do you work for?"

The man looked up at him and, through clenched teeth, said, "Fat Gator," and died.

Clint had no idea who Fat Gator was. He wondered if Roper would.

Outside of El Paso, several days later, Henry "Fat Gator" Miller read a Denver newspaper, which carried the account of the events that had led to the death of his twins. Others died, too, but he was only concerned with the twins. Obviously, he had sent them on too hard a task, and they weren't ready for it. His intended robbery for Denver would have to wait, as would his chance to cross swords with Talbot Roper. As for Clint Adams, he doubted he'd come in contact with him again.

He folded the newspaper and put it aside. He was going to have to find himself another set of "twins."

Watch for

DEAD HORSE CANYON

224th novel in the exciting GUNSMITH series
from Jove

Coming in August!

J. R. ROBERTS
THE GUNSMITH